THE HIDDEN CHILD

THE
BRIDGE
BETWEEN
WORLDS

MK SHEVLIN

THE BRIDGE BETWEEN WORLDS
M.K. Shevlin
Copyright © 2022 M.K. Shevlin
All rights reserved.

Hardcover print book ISBN: 979-8-9869277-1-8
Paperback print book ISBN: 979-8-9869277-0-1
Digital online ISBN: 979-8-986277-2-5

This book is a work of fiction. Names, characters, places and incidents are products of the author's imagination or are used fictitiously. Any resemblance to actual persons, living or dead, events or locations is entirely coincidental.

Dedication

For
my nephew
Logan

Incredible man
Incredible firefighter
Incredible everything

Gone far too soon…

Table of Contents

Foreword i

Chapter 1 – The Escape 1

Chapter 2 – Theresa and Melody 5

Chapter 3 – Miss Medlock 13

Chapter 4 – Harbingers and Kettles 15

Chapter 5 – Old Man Turly 21

Chapter 6 – Theresa's Loss 25

Chapter 7 – Friends 29

Chapter 8 – Mina's New Clothes 33

Chapter 9 – Stitches and Lemon Juice 37

Chapter 10 – Escape from Bart's 43

Chapter 11 – Woods Elves and Mermaids 49

Chapter 12 – Books and Friendship 53

Chapter 13 – Unicorns and the Henhouse 55

Chapter 14 – The Boxcar 59

Chapter 15 – Talking to the Birds 63

Chapter 16 – Haggis 67

Chapter 17 – Sleeping Mermaid 69

Chapter 18 – Melody's Diagnosis 71

Chapter 19 – Manchester Retrieval 75

Chapter 20 – The Pilot and the Curse 79

Chapter 21 – The Dream Realised 81

Chapter 22 – The Deconstruction of Mina 85

Chapter 23 – The Fearsome Child 91

Chapter 24 – Elbry House 95

Table of Contents

Chapter 25 – The Siren's Song......99
Chapter 26 – Seeking Redemption......109
Chapter 27 – Crossley......113
Chapter 28 – Settled In......115
Chapter 29 – Icy Roads and Mr Wallace......119
Chapter 30 – Stops Along the Way......125
Chapter 31 – Mr Fix-it......131
Chapter 32 – The Meat Locker......139
Chapter 33 – Turly's House......147
Chapter 34 – The Scar......149
Chapter 35 – Medlock and Turly......153
Chapter 36 – Katie's Coffee......155
Chapter 37 – The Predators and the Prey......159
Chapter 38 – An Unexpected Ally......161
Chapter 39 – The Stranger in the Darkness......169
Chapter 40 – Tom and Jimmy......171
Chapter 41 – Confrontation and Breakfast......173
Chapter 42 – A Good Night's Sleep......177
Chapter 43 – Nightmare Road......181
Chapter 44 – The Cave......189
Chapter 45 – Dance of Shadows......199
Chapter 46 – Final Words......203
Chapter 47 – The Dark Day......205
Acknowledgements......211

Foreword

Whilst this book is categorised as a fantasy/folklore novel in bookstores and online, who's to say it isn't actually a historical biography?

Who's to say these events didn't actually happen long ago, possibly in another reality? That these characters weren't real and their journeys were not shared by sentient trees with those who have open hearts and minds?

Not me... don't you know.

MK Shevlin

Chapter One

The Escape

A RAINDROP MADE a slight *tap* sound as it hit the dirty windowpane. It trickled down the glass before resting on the windowsill.

Nearby and in the distance, random rapid-fire explosions sounded, dwarfed by a sudden and loud clap of thunder overhead. After an ominous pause, the sky opened up, drenching the entire area. Several flashes of lightning revealed the devastation; the large four-story building had been reduced to rubble. The building, which had housed the windowpane, was only a charred shell now, two partial walls standing adjacent to each other in the darkness, supported only by the cracked and decaying mortar between their bricks.

Shattered glass and debris blanketed the area. The once beautiful and ornate iron fence that surrounded the estate was now a gnarled mass, beyond repair or recognition. Burned clothing, books, and a child's doll, its face melted and charred, were being submerged in the muddy rain. Nearby, several motorcars lay on their sides, disfigured, blackened, and smouldering from the fires that had engulfed them hours earlier.

A moment later, the remains of the building collapsed to the ground like a mudslide in the spring, creating a tidal wave of bricks and debris toppling off the edge of the ancient stone foundation. Flashes of lightning revealed a child's hand buried under the broken bricks. The delicate hand lay motionless as the rain washed away the grime and blood, but after several moments, a single finger twitched. The final clap of thunder roared overhead, shaking the ground.

The hand moved again, now forcefully. Fumbling and scraping, the child frantically pushed the last of the bricks from her path and crawled to the surface, only to land face-first into the muddy water, where she lay motionless for a long moment, then rose to her feet, struggling to keep her balance in the treacherous mud and debris.

She lifted her eyes to the dark sky, her face relaxing for a moment as heavy raindrops hit her forehead and cheeks, taking some of the mud and blood with them as they worked their way downward and vanished onto the wet ground.

The girl was thin and smaller than most eleven-year-olds. Her long, light brown hair was matted against her head and face. She had a certain prettiness to her, though one would never know it for all the mud, cuts, and bruises to her face.

She staggered in the darkness through the debris, the only light coming from brief flashes of bombs impacting on the horizon as the thunderstorm now moved off to the east. The girl tripped and stumbled over a wooden doorframe, chunks of broken concrete, a crushed tricycle, and the charred remains of a human body.

Just above her, a barrage balloon was in its final death throes. Still clinging to its steel cable, which was tethered to the remains of a nearby building, it twisted, groaned, and writhed as angry flames enveloped it. Burning embers danced around her like bottle flies, enjoying their brief lives and then falling to the ground in a sizzling finale.

The child hardly heard the surrounding impacts, not because they were far away but because an explosion had ruptured her left eardrum. Her ear was encrusted with dried blood, and a thick, clear liquid seeped down the side of her ghostly pale face and neck. A loud hiss echoed in her right ear.

Her left shoe was nowhere to be seen, but she didn't seem to notice its absence. Her torn and tattered clothes were covered in mud and her own blood, and with one hand she clutched at an old silver door key that hung from a chain about her neck while fumbling in her skirt pocket to make certain her little pile of acorns was still there.

The child had been living at Saint Austin's Orphanage for many years.

All that remained of it now was a smouldering pile of debris. She saw no other children. She saw no one at all. Her entire body began trembling, and her eyes grew wide and darted all about.

"Hell… hello?" she cried out in a weak, quivering voice. "Hello? Anyone there? Any…one?"

The girl realised they were gone. They were all gone, and she was alone. The sky soon grew quiet.

A dull pain reached into her mind as she stumbled about in the darkness. Her right leg wasn't moving very well at all and felt heavy and slow to respond to her will. A sudden image of lightning reflected in a large shard of glass buried deep in her right thigh. In disbelief, she stared for a moment at the shard and the wound it had caused.

Wrapping her small, dirty hand around it, she pulled it out, slicing the inside of her fingers and palm on the edges of the sharp glass. The girl stared at her leg, open-mouthed, as if surprised it didn't hurt more. As the glass fell from her hand and shattered on the ground, she watched her palm fill with blood that almost looked black in the flickering darkness. She fell to her knees and vomited bile from her empty stomach several times, her entire body shaking violently. After several moments, the nausea passed. She gathered herself and used several torn sections of her skirt to wrap her hand and leg to stem the bleeding. She stumbled onto the street as the fiery barrage balloon crashed down upon the remains of the orphanage, silhouetting her in a huge fireball.

The storm had now passed off to the east. London was silent. In the faint moonlight breaking through the clouds, she noticed an intact bottle of milk on Mrs Melman's front porch. The house had been levelled, but the milk, no doubt delivered the day prior, somehow survived. With trembling hands, she picked it up, removed the cork, and drank from it, much of it running down her neck and chest. The girl hadn't eaten or drunk anything in nearly two days.

She sat on the porch and wept. Where were the rest of the children? Where were the adults? Were they *all* gone? She would even welcome the sight and shrill voice of Miss Medlock, the headmistress, right now. The girl and the rest of the children were to have been relocated to the countryside a week ago, but their transportation broke down, and the German air raids destroyed the main roadways, preventing the replacement motorcar parts from being delivered.

Her head and leg throbbed, and every step felt as though she were walking through water. The girl wandered into the darkness, cradling the blood-covered bottle to her heart.

Morning had come. The cobblestone street had given way long ago to this country dirt road that seemed to go on forever. The ground and air were still damp from rain, and the stench of smoke burned in her lungs as she stumbled and swayed from exhaustion and pain. Her head and body pounded with every beat of her angry heart. The blood covering her leg had begun to flake off, and some had run down into her remaining shoe, making a *squish* sound with every other step. Scarcely a single thought entered her mind in many hours, but though her body was shutting down, she kept moving.

She had to keep moving.

2 Chapter Two

Theresa and Melody

THERESA BUSIED HERSELF outside her cottage, sweeping the muddy rain and dead leaves from her front porch with a tattered broom. She hummed an old tune that she had known from as far back as she could remember but never seemed to recall all of it or even how she knew it. She paused for a moment to take a puff off her cigarette and a sip from her teacup, which was balanced precariously on one of the two rocking chairs near the front door. She tucked her hair behind her ears, shooed the cat out of the way, and then began sweeping again.

After a moment, she spotted something moving out of the corner of her eye. She turned her head and gasped as an icy chill ran up her spine, the cigarette dropping from her mouth. In the distance, she saw what appeared to be the ghost of a young girl, deathly white and covered in blood. The woman closed her eyes and mumbled to herself, "It's all in your head. There's no such thing as ghosts. Get a grip, Theresa. She's not real. She's not here. She can't be here. There is no such thing as ghosts." She opened her eyes. The child was still there, staggering down the gravel road. This was no ghost.

"Melody!" Theresa screamed back toward the house as she began running to the girl, nearly tripping over the broom as she tossed it out of her way.

The child saw the woman running toward her as the milk bottle slipped from her grasp and shattered on the ground, spattering her bare, bloodied legs. All went dark as she collapsed onto the dirt road.

She opened her eyes for a moment to see the woman hovering over her. Her vision was blurred and distorted, and she couldn't understand the faint, echoing words the woman was saying. All went dark again.

"Mummy? Mummy, please don't hurt me! Please don't hurt me! I'll be good! I promise! Please don't hurt me!" the child pleaded in a weak, fearful voice when she awoke much later.

"Shhh. It's all right, honey. No one is going to hurt you. I'm here to help. Just relax." A distant but gentle voice dispelled the silence.

She looked about and realised she was now lying in a soft bed. Her senses were suddenly wide-awake. Pain enveloped her entire body. She watched in silence as the woman finished cleaning and dressing her leg wound. The woman was pretty, with big brown eyes and shoulder-length brown hair. She shared a smile with the child.

"I'm Melody. What's your name?" the woman asked.

"Um… Mina," she answered with a quivering voice, straining to understand the woman's words.

"Mina? That's a pretty name. Mina, you've been hurt. Try to stay still. You're going to be fine. There. All done." Melody shared another smile as she removed a pair of blood-covered rubber gloves with a *snap*.

Shortly, another woman entered the room with a pot of tea and a wedge of bread with a bit of jam on it served on a small tin tray.

"This is Theresa, Mina. She's the one who found you," Melody said. "She brought you some breakfast! Can you try to sit up?"

With a bit of help from Melody, Mina managed a sitting position. She devoured the bread and tea in silence but soon surrendered to the wave of exhaustion crashing over her.

Some hours later, Mina opened her heavy eyes to see Melody sitting next to her on the bed with strange rubber tubes hanging from her ears.

The woman was moving something cold and metallic around on her chest, deep in thought and listening intently. Mina's eyes moved about the room and toward the dark window. *It must be night*, she thought. She had to force her eyes open, but after every few seconds, she would find them closing again. She repeated this cycle many times as she watched the silent woman next to her. Eventually Melody removed the cold object from her chest and pulled the black tubes from her ears, which seemed to have crooked spouts of metal attached at the ends. The woman smiled at her and stroked her face.

"I was listening to your heart, honey."

Mina scarcely heard a word she said, for the loud hiss still echoing in her head. She felt more like a witness to the events surrounding her than the subject. The woman examined the lumps and old scars on her collarbone and forearm, using her fingers to explore every inch of her bones beneath her skin. A sudden wave of sadness covered Melody's face, tears forming in her eyes. Mina knew what she had found.

Melody lifted Mina's hand to examine her bandaged palm. She could see a bit of blood still seeping through the gauze, but the woman seemed pleased. She then inspected the tips of Mina's fingers. On the first joint of her fingers were round, swollen knots. Mina winced a bit as Melody rolled them between her thumb and index finger. Their eyes met at her reaction. She laid Mina's hand back down, giving it several gentle pats. Mina watched as the woman let out a deep sigh of concern and lowered her eyes. Melody pulled the covers back up to her chin, giving her cheek a gentle caress. After a moment, Mina felt her eyes close.

The following day brought much the same; Melody would wake her every few hours to tend to her injuries and offer her a bite to eat and drink. Mina was awake only long enough to eat the meals: eggs, hard bread with jam or a bit of mince, and a glass of fresh goat's milk. Through her blurred vision, she would occasionally see Theresa standing at the doorway, staring at her, arms folded. Mina would fall back into a deep sleep without speaking a single word.

It was on the second night when Mina awoke from a horrible dream to the sound of air-raid sirens in the distance. In the dream, she witnessed the impact of a bomb striking the roadway in front of a motorcar whose headlamps weren't shielded properly. The car swerved to avoid the crater created by the bomb but failed, rolling into it, sending its occupants—a mother and her two children—headfirst into the windscreen. After several moments, a small boy crawled from the fiery wreckage. "Mummy! Mummy!" the child cried out in horror.

Mina bolted up in bed, her heart racing, and cried out again, "Mummy!" The sound of hurried footsteps approached the closed door. Panting, she shielded her eyes from the light of the other room as Melody entered the doorway.

"Hi, sleepyhead!" the woman exclaimed with a big smile. "How are you feeling?"

"Where... where am I?"

"You're in our home. You're safe here, Mina. You've had quite an ordeal. Can you talk about it?" Melody spoke quickly, and Mina struggled to understand and keep up with the woman for the hissing and ringing in her ear.

"I can't... I can't hear you very well," Mina said, feeling the gauze packing and sticking plaster on her left ear with her fingers. "I can't hear myself either!" Mina's eyes flooded with tears as she began hyperventilating. Melody sat down next to her, placing her hand on Mina's shoulder and then checking her racing pulse.

"Mina, you've been hurt."

The child's eyes darted around the dark room, scarcely hearing a word Melody spoke. The woman grasped her by the chin, looking her squarely in the eyes.

"Watch my mouth," she said sternly, but with gentleness in her eyes. "You are going to have to learn to read lips. Mina, I'm a nurse. I work with injured people all the time. Your left eardrum has been ruptured, and your right ear has been damaged as well. If you watch my mouth, it will help you understand what I'm saying, okay?"

The girl's tears filled Melody's palm as she nodded in silence.

"What happened to you?" Melody asked again.

"I'm... I was in Saint Austin's when the building fell down on top of me. I..."

Her voice dropped off as her mind revisited the scene; she remembered the building shaking violently, the horrible sound of the sirens blaring and of the bombs impacting all around her. She remembered the terror she felt running up the old wooden stairs from the cellar as the rock walls on either side of her collapsed inward, rapidly blocking her escape. As she fled toward the main entrance, an ear-shattering explosion and earthquake-like jolt struck the building, twisting and crumpling it into a pile of debris.

She had just reached the doorway and looked up to the sky when the brick archway above her collapsed, burying her alive and alone. She remembered the endless silence and the pain she felt. Then she remembered no more until the rain and shaking earth woke her.

Her thoughts turned to her friends Hilary, Katie, and Mr Turly. Were they alive? Did they get out of the building in time?

"So you're an orphan," Melody said, bringing the child back to the moment. "Austin's is in London, a long, long way from here, honey. Did you walk all this way?" Melody asked, as the small girl stared off into space, lost deep in her own thoughts and the emptiness she felt within.

"Are you okay?" Melody asked, a look of concern covering her face.

The woman spun her head toward the doorway as though she had heard a sound and smiled.

"Theresa's home with dinner! Can you walk a little… out to the kitchen? Will you try?" Melody asked.

"I am feeling a bit peckish, miss," she said, trying very hard to be pleasant though she felt quite the contrary.

Melody folded the blankets back for the child. Mina looked down at the oversized nightgown she was now wearing with a look of confusion on her face. Melody lifted Mina's chin toward her.

"I'm sorry, honey. Your own clothes were ruined. We had to put you into something clean and proper. I hope you don't mind."

Mina nodded, checking for her necklace that held an old silver door key. She fondled it for a moment in relief.

"No, miss. That's quite fine. My acorns?"

"Your acorns are in a little bowl on the dresser. They are quite safe," Melody said with a reassuring smile.

"May I use your loo first?"

"Of course!" Melody helped her to her feet, and the child started making the bed.

"Leave it, Mina. I'll take care of it," she said with a smile.

Melody supported her as she shuffled out from the dark bedroom. Mina winced in pain, feeling quite dizzy. A wave of nausea filled her stomach. Though the deep wound had been neatly stitched up by Melody, her leg felt heavy and throbbed with each step. She could again feel her heart pounding in her chest. Melody walked her to the loo, helped her do her business and clean up a bit, and then into the kitchen.

"I have dinner!" Theresa announced. "I found a bit of bread and cheese in the Cabots' house whilst they were in their shelter. They won't miss it. Old Lady Cabot had chucked it in the bin. Such a waste..." Theresa stopped as she turned and saw Mina standing next to Melody.

In silence, Theresa sliced the mouldy sections off the bread and cheese as Melody helped Mina settle into a chair. Mina couldn't help but notice the energy had shifted in the room.

The meal was modest but filling. Mr Pims, the women's rather scrawny tuxedo cat, seemed pleased with his little meal too. He purred much of the remaining evening, taking great interest in Mina, venturing up to her and rubbing his face and body against her feet dangling from the chair. Mina quite liked the cheerful soul. She found the bizarre vibration his body made comforting.

So many thoughts and questions filled Mina's mind about the fate of her friends, but they would have to wait as she was already growing so sleepy. She hardly spoke during dinner and felt out of place in the home of the strangers as they chatted during their meal about the death of Mrs Cartwright and her son Michael, whose motorcar had slid into a bomb crater, killing them both. The only survivor was her young son, Timothy, as his father had also been recently killed on the front lines. But Mina already knew about it from her dream... She had witnessed it; she had felt them die.

Mina studied Theresa in silence. Theresa had a kind but scarred face. A red line ran from the left side of her cheek to her mouth, resembling a long red zipper. She looked as though she had lived a difficult life. Despite the disfiguring scar, she was still quite pretty. Streaks of grey ran through her once all-blond hair, and a wearied sadness filled her eyes. Mina noted that Theresa hadn't looked at her even once or acknowledged her presence.

Melody and Theresa, whilst talking about their day, hadn't noticed the girl slump over and land face-first on her dinner plate, fast asleep.

Melody carried the girl back to the bedroom with Theresa following behind.

"Tree, could you at least pull back the covers for her?" Melody said, an obvious hint of irritation in her whisper. Theresa silently complied. She showed no emotion on her face at all. Melody gently covered the child with a warm blanket.

Melody exited the room without a word. Theresa remained in the doorway for a long moment. This little girl looked so very much like another child she once knew. Her eyes filled with tears as she found herself lost in old memories. She shook them away, closing the door behind her.

3 Chapter Three

Miss Medlock

AT THE SCENE of Saint Austin's, Miss Medlock's icy veneer was melting like a block of ice on a hot July day. The aged but prim and proper headmistress of Saint Austin's looked ruffled and mussed. Her white blouse was covered in dirt and mud. Her hair looked tussled and was falling out of the dozen or so hairpins that held it in place. She stood, arms folded, watching the men dig through the rubble with spades and bare hands. She looked to the sky as the dark clouds moved in with the promise of more rain.

To date, twenty-three children and six adults were confirmed dead from the attack. Fourteen children and four adults were still unaccounted for.

A rare tear welled up in her eye, but she shook it away. Even the thought of that odd Mina being buried in this rubble grieved her, especially as her last words to the child were hateful and cruel. Three days before German bombers levelled the orphanage, Medlock had watched Mina coaxing Jenny, an annoying Irish child with ginger hair, to the backside of the orphanage grounds where an old stone wall had been forbidden for the children to play on as it was crumbling and dangerous.

Medlock had noticed the girls from her office window, but she was simply too busy to be bothered with the two misfits. After a moment of tedious paperwork, she turned her eyes and ears back to the two girls wandering up and down the length of the wall unnoticed by the rest of the orphanage staff; she would have words with them about it.

The girls chatted, giggled, and sang songs in a strange language that Mina had taught Jenny, though Jenny understood none of the words. Medlock even caught herself smiling at the sound of Mina's laughter; she had never heard the child laugh before and only rarely seen her smile. Suddenly a section of the old wall gave way under Jenny's feet, and the ginger-haired girl tumbled some ten feet to the ground into the wild brush. Several stones followed her, knocking her unconscious. Fortunately, Jenny only suffered a minor concussion and skin abrasions, but Medlock overreacted to what Mina had done and used the wooden paddle from her office on her.

She replayed her harsh words to Mina over and over in her mind, wishing she could take them back. Mina was a strange child, but Medlock didn't wish her any harm. She had been at Saint Austin's for as long as Medlock could remember and never seemed to age. The other children grew up around her, but Mina always seemed the same, stuck in time at the age of eleven. She found the situation disturbing but refused to let her mind delve any deeper into it.

The digging pace slowed. Several of the men rested their heads on the handle of their spades. It had been five days since the air raid levelled Saint Austin's, and the exhausted men were losing hope.

"Oi! Back to work, you lot! Time is of the essence!" Medlock barked out, using common slang that was anathema to the prim and proper headmistress. She looked again at the darkening sky. Once the rain started, the chance of finding anyone else alive would be doused.

All the men picked up the pace with their spades except Turly. The old man, his unruly white hair matted to his sweat-drenched head, stood staring down at something in the pile of bricks.

"Turly! Get a move on!" Medlock commanded.

The old man stood, unmoved. She approached him to see what had caught his interest. Medlock gasped as she saw what Turly unearthed. A child's shoe was in the rubble, a left shoe. Mina's shoe.

4 Chapter four

Harbingers and Kettles

WHOP, WHOP, WHOP!

Mina awoke to Mr Pims's paw whopping her nose. The cat scurried off as she sat up, startled, on her little makeshift bed near the wood-burning stove. The bed they made for her was comfortable and warm through much of the night until the fire grew cold, but it was morning now.

She shivered. Her right leg felt stiff and bruised. Mina tucked her long brown hair behind her little pointed ears, revealing a still-crusted blood clot, which continued leaking from her silent left ear. She lifted her gigantic sleeping gown to check the dressing on her leg. The wound was healing nicely now, with only a small reddish-yellow spot seeping through the gauze.

She guessed it was morning as she could see small streams of light through tiny holes in the black window cloth. She looked around the corner of the living room wall into the kitchen. Four average-sized houseplants sat on the windowsill above the kitchen sink, seeking the morning light. They were a pretty red colour with oddly shaped leaves and purple flowers. They smelled good, like spice. Several antique copper kettles sat on a shelf as decorations, and photographs of American soldiers and Indians from the 1860s in assorted frames covered the wall to her left. A ceramic chicken sat on the counter, staring at her. Mina wondered if there were any biscuits in it.

She faintly heard a rooster crowing somewhere in the distance. It reminded her of when she would walk down to the chicken house and gather eggs for Miss Hatchet, the cook, at Saint Austin's. Mina would carry an empty basket and return with it filled with freshly laid eggs. Miss Hatchet would always give her a slice of bacon or hard bread with mince on it for her help as long as she didn't break any of the eggs. So she was quite careful loading the basket as the little treat made her feel special.

Mr Pims was clawing his way up the black cloth covering the living room window when it gave way with a crash, shattering a clay pot that sat on the small table below. The morning light flooded the room. Mr Pims let out a loud yowl and then scampered off behind the sofa to hide.

Mina squinted in the bright light that suddenly flooded the room; the sun was actually shining. She hadn't seen the sun in nearly a month with all the London rain. The sun slid behind the blackening clouds, taking much of the morning light with it. Something caught Mina's eye on the inset window bay: six tall plants in terracotta pots. Still hobbling, she made her way over to investigate them. Mina's eyes grew wide at her discovery. *Harbingers!* She had never known anyone dare to keep harbingers in their home. A wave of fear filled her.

"How dangerous is this?" she mused aloud to herself. They were quite beautiful and colourful. Yellow, purple, red, and some variegated harbingers she had never seen before. Mina sensed a presence behind her. Quite startled, she turned to see Theresa.

"Do you like my orchids?"

"I didn't pull the cloth down! It was Mr Pims. I swear. Please don't punish me. Please… Please don't hurt me!" Mina pleaded with a quivering voice, taking several steps backward.

Theresa pinched her eyebrows together. "Whoa! I would never hurt you, child. Why would you say that? Has someone hurt you?"

Mina's mouth moved slightly, as though she were about to answer, but after a moment, she pressed her lips together, dropping her eyes in silence.

Theresa took a deep breath. "I know Mr Pims pulled the black cloth down. He does it several times a week, and I just put it back up. Cats are like that."

"I… I didn't know that. Mr Pims is the first cat I have ever met proper. Oh, by the way, what's Mr Pims's first name? Would he mind if I addressed him by his first name?" Mina rambled nervously.

"His first name is Mister, and he prefers to have his full name used, and I will never hurt you, Mina. So relax!" Theresa said in a long, single breath.

After a moment of silence, Mina spoke. "Orchids?"

"They're lovely, aren't they?" Theresa asked.

Mina nodded. "We call them *harbingers*. You should free them, straightaway. It's quite dangerous to capture them, don't you know, and you tied them up on sticks! I don't think they like that!" Her voice cracked in horror.

Theresa looked at the little girl curiously.

"I grow them, child. They are my favourite houseplant. Why are you afraid of them?"

Mina stood silent with wide eyes, studying the tethered harbingers. "Where… where are their faces? They 'aven't any faces!"

"If you use your imagination, you can see them. Look," Theresa said, pointing to a particular orange-and-yellow bloom. "If you look real hard, you can see its nose and its mouth and where its eyes would be."

"No! No! They have proper faces! Harbingers have proper faces! Where are their faces?" Mina's voice climbed nearly an octave to a near-shrieking pitch.

"Let's have a cup of tea," Theresa suggested with a condescending smile. "You can tell me all about harbingers over morning tea."

Mina followed Theresa into the kitchen. The woman drew some fresh water and lit the stove. A sizzling sound could be heard as a few drops of water rolled down the copper kettle onto the flame of the gas stove.

Mina studied the photographs on the wall in silence. "Are these people your family, miss?"

Theresa looked at the old photographs and then back at Mina. "No. They're not my family."

"That man has a fluty thing just like yours!" Mina said, pointing to a particular brave with a flute hanging over his shoulder.

Theresa nodded, her hard veneer toward the child cracking ever so slightly.

"Are they friends of yours, miss?"

"No, I don't know any of them. They all have been gone for a very long—"

"Where did they all go? Are they on holiday?"

"They all died many, many years ago. I don't know any of their names except for one. The first photo on the top left, his name is Chief Black Kettle."

"Is that why you collect kettles… because of him? Did he invent kettles?"

"No, child, he didn't invent kettles. These photographs are from the American Civil War, which happened around eighty years ago in another country, America. Have you heard of the United States of America?"

Mina nodded. "My friend Hilary talks about America all the time!"

"Is she from America?"

"No, she's from Lincolnshire."

"Oh. Well, Melody is originally from America. Did you know that? A place called California."

Mina shook her head. "No, miss. I didn't!"

"Anyway… There was a war, a terrible war in which many people were killed," Theresa said, pointing to the photograph of Chief Black Kettle. "This man was an Indian chief who tried to make peace with the American armies and in the end was betrayed and his people slaughtered."

"Oh, how horrible!" Mina said with wide eyes. "Were you there?"

"No, child. I'm not *that* old." Theresa looked deep into the photograph for a moment. "There is just something I find fascinating about this time period. Something…"

"So he didn't invent the kettle?" Mina asked again.

"No, he didn't invent the kettle," Theresa said, finally sharing a smile with her. They looked at the photos in silence as the kettle rumbled on the stove.

Mina looked up at Theresa with tears in her eyes. "My people are at war too. I think that's why they sent me here, to hide me and keep me safe. I think that's why they sent you, to look after me until it's time for us to both go home."

Theresa pinched her eyebrows together and cocked her head slightly at Mina in silence as the kettle began whistling.

Melody shuffled in from the bedroom, wrapping her dressing gown about her waist, with her hair mussed about and her slippers *scuff-scuffing* as she approached the kitchen table. She squinted from the bright light, knowing instinctively that Mr Pims had been climbing the window cloth again.

"Mel, Mina was about to tell us about orchids—harbingers, as she calls them," Theresa said as the dishevelled woman plopped down in her chair at the table, looking half-asleep and in need of a cup of tea or, better yet, coffee.

"Oh?" Melody responded, only half listening as Theresa poured her tea.

Mina seized the opportunity and began.

"Harbingers tell us things," she said, leaning forward on the kitchen table toward Theresa, looking and sounding sincere. "Every colour is a warning. They grow in the forest, mostly on the trees, and we try not to make them angry or step on them; they don't like that."

Melody was now wide-awake. She sipped her tea, holding the cup with both hands, listening intently.

"What do they tell you, Mina?" she asked as she shared a glance with Theresa.

"If they are yellow, that means the forest is happy. If rain is coming, they turn blue. Red means a good harvest, but if they turn black, well, that's very bad, don't you know. It's dangerous to keep harbingers in your house. Everyone knows that unless they're simpletons. You don't want to make them angry!"

"Mina, they're just houseplants," Theresa said flatly. "Orchids are just houseplants. They never change colour. The blue ones are always blue, the yellow ones are always yellow, and black ones are extremely rare, though I've never actually seen one. They are just plants, and I'm not a simpleton!"

"No, miss. They are dangerous!" Mina insisted with wide eyes. "You should free them straightaway!"

Melody, seeing Mina's growing anxiety and Theresa's irritation, interrupted them both.

"Maybe harbingers are dangerous where you come from, but here, they are just orchids, pretty flowers. Trust us. Theresa has been growing them for many years. They are safe here. She protects and cares for them. They hold no ill will toward anyone."

Mina sat back in her chair, looking relieved. "Well, that's good then," she said matter-of-factly.

"So um, Mina," Melody said, trying to change the subject, "tell me about the acorns that we found in your pocket. Do they mean something special to you?"

"They bring good luck! If you put them in your windowsills, they will keep you safe," Mina replied.

"That's kind of an old wives' tale, isn't it?" Melody asked.

"No, it's true, especially if they are sprinkled with fairy dust like mine are, though most of the dust has come off. That's probably why the building fell on me, don't you know."

Melody smiled at Mina's convictions and innocence. She looked over at Theresa, who seemed to be doing the same. It was rare to see her smiling. After a moment, she saw Theresa's smile fade and an empty expression cover her face. She had gone into the darkness.

5 Chapter Five

Old Man Turly

TURLY STRUGGLED TURNING the key to the shed with his old, gnarled hands, his spade leaning against his ribs. The promised heavy rain had begun, making the key slippery to grasp. The door creaked open as he gave it a shove. After fumbling about in the darkness for a moment, he found the pull chain to the overhead light bulb and gave it a yank. Dim light filled the shed, revealing an assortment of neatly ordered tools.

The old man placed his spade next to the other stack of tools leaning against the sidewall and gathered his walking cane in its stead, hanging it over his wrist. He looked down at his blistered hands filled with splinters from the weathered handle of the spade. He tried to close them, but they were too swollen to make a proper fist. He reached into his coat pocket and pulled out the shoe he'd retrieved in the rubble earlier that day. Mina's shoe. He knew it was hers as he had given them to her just a few months ago as a gift. Much of the clothing provided to the children by the orphanage were hand-me-downs from donations of various local charities. Mina's shoes were old and three sizes too big for her feet, so the old man had purchased a new pair for her out of his wages. He remembered how grateful the child was when he presented them to her. He relived the moment in his mind, her smile and gratitude for the gift.

Turly looked over toward his workshop table at the bit of wood that he had partially carved for her. It was going to be a unicorn. He regretted he hadn't found time to finish it and give it to her. His eyes then moved to the corkboard above the table and the two dozen or so pictures that the child had drawn for him with crayon and paper over the years. He still had every drawing. As he lowered his knackered body into the wooden chair at the workbench, his eyes filled with tears as he studied each of them in turn. They were drawings of forests, unicorns, mermaids, elves. Mina always included herself in the middle of the picture with a smile. On most of the drawings, she'd written a little note, saying things like:

Thank you for being my friend, Mr Turly. You are a very nice man, Mr Turly. Thank you for my new shoes, Mr Turly! They are so lovely. Or *Thank you for the boiled sweets! They were yumz!*

He thought back to when he first met the foundling. It was springtime, long ago.

Turly had spent several hours walking the grounds, picking up rubbish that had accumulated, preparing to cut the grass, when he noticed a brown bottle with a rolled-up piece of paper inserted into the neck and tucked into a hedge.

He stooped over and retrieved the bottle. After slicking his wild greying hair back, he unrolled the note.

It read:

I am so alone and so far from home.

I have no friends.

I have no one to love me.

I have no one to talk to.

Please help me.

If you find this, I love you.

M.

The writing was that of a child and, judging by its lack of weathering, had been written recently. The old man spent the next few days observing the windows of Saint Austin's as he did his grounds work.

One drizzly afternoon, his eyes fell upon a child, a young girl sitting by the window of her room whilst the other children played on the playground. She appeared to be sitting in a wooden chair alone with her face pressed upon the glass. The girl stared out at the trees and sky, her eyes not focused on anything in particular. He studied her for a moment, his heart going out to her, knowing from personal experience the emptiness she was feeling. Eventually the girl glanced down. When their eyes met, Turly raised his hand, holding her note between two fingers, and smiled at the child. After a moment, she smiled and waved.

As the night descended, the rain pounding the old shed, Turly sat in silence, his only companion a half bottle of scotch and his old pipe. He looked at the strange engravings on the base of the pipe and then looked to Mina's bottle note pinned to the corkboard; they were in the same language. The old man wept silently as he cradled the shoe in his hands.

Chapter Six

Theresa's Loss

THERESA ASCENDED THE rickety fold-down ladder in the kitchen to the attic. She lit a small oil lamp, which hung from a support beam, lifted it from its hook, and placed it on an overturned wine barrel next to her.

After a long pause and a deep breath, she unlatched and opened the lid of her dusty hope chest. It creaked as the lid locked into place. She hadn't opened this box of memories in over ten years. She knelt, staring into it, as memories flooded her mind. To the right lay a small stack of black-and-white photographs. Theresa lifted the dusty memories out and held them for a moment before removing the long piece of yellow ribbon that bound them together. She studied the old ribbon in her hand. A knot in the middle held several captive strands of long blond hair. Theresa caressed the hairs with her fingers before carefully draping the ribbon over her wrist. She seated herself cross-legged on the wooden attic floor. Theresa took another deep breath as she began flipping through the photographs one by one. Her bottom lip quivered, and her hands trembled.

The pictures were of a young girl and herself, taken many years ago. Theresa stared at the features of her then scar-free face. She had forgotten what she looked like without the deep red line that now ran along her cheek. She had forgotten how young she once was and so full of life. Her eyes moved to the smiling child in her arms. The girl looked exactly like a younger version of herself, the eyes, the blond hair, the smile, the high cheekbones. She turned the photo over.

Theresa and Lucy

3 July 1926.

The second photo was of Lucy laughing whilst a droopy-lipped bloodhound licked her face. The next was one of herself pushing the happy child in a tree swing. In her mind, the photograph began to move and was suddenly filled with vivid colour, the bright yellow blouse, the brown skirt, and even the varying shades of blond in the little girl's hair. Theresa remembered that moment with such clarity that she could even hear Lucy laughing and giggling as she kept saying, *Higher, Mummy! Higher!* Theresa wondered if her daughter would have still looked like her had she lived to be an adult.

She shook her head several times as though trying to shake the memory away, for the perfume of pain that accompanied it was overwhelming even now. After a moment, she could take no more and rebound the photographs, placing them back in their proper place in the locker. Theresa wiped the tears from her eyes with the sleeve of her jumper.

A small pile of children's clothes, a black woollen peacoat, and a pair of children's boots lay neatly folded to the left of the photographs. An old hand-made rag doll lay next to the clothes. Theresa lifted them out with great care, her eyes revisiting every inch of them. With closed eyes, she buried her nose into them, inhaling deeply; they still smelled of the child. She again looked at the top photograph in the locker; Lucy was wearing the very same yellow blouse that was atop the pile of clothes she now held in her arms. A tidal wave of emotion rolled over her, drowning her in sorrow. Theresa began sobbing. She rocked back and forth, cradling the clothes and doll in her arms as the last drop from the oil lamp burned and swallowed her into darkness.

Melody waited patiently in the kitchen for Theresa to return from the attic. It had been nearly an hour. Theresa had promised it would only take five minutes. Melody knew better.

Eventually Theresa descended the wooden ladder, holding the clothes, boots, and rag doll close to her heart. Her face was red and swollen. Refusing to give Melody eye contact, she set the precious items on the corner of the kitchen table.

She stared at the doll, obviously debating something in her mind. After a long moment, she regathered it, looked about the kitchen, and carefully hid the rag doll atop a cupboard, just out of view.

Melody rose and poured Theresa a cup of tea, squeezing her shoulder as Theresa, her hands still shaking, lit a cigarette. They sat in silence as the grieving woman sipped her tea and stared blankly at the table before her. After she had regained her composure, she called out loudly toward the bedroom, "Mina, could you come in here for a moment? I have some things for you."

Chapter Seven

Friends

HREE OF THE surviving children from St Austin's were transported to Saint Bartholomew's Hospital. Bart's, as it was known, was in Smithfield, London. It was over eight hundred years old. Numerous soldiers were at Bart's as well, packed in tightly, as the war had caused so many injuries. Bart's was also a target from above and had suffered much damage.

Hilary, a thin young girl of twelve from Lincolnshire with mousy blond hair and fair, freckled skin, received only a foot laceration, but the wound had gone septic and required her to be put in hospital to clear it up. She had lost her father to cancer when she was eight and her mother to tuberculosis when she was ten and had been living at Saint Austin's since that time. Hilary realised it would be almost impossible for her to be adopted, not only because of her age but during a time of war, so she held out little hope of finding a proper family. Hilary would often read about America and hoped one day to move there and start a new life. She longed for a place where the sun shone more often and she wouldn't have to contend with the almost daily rain.

Despite repeated warnings from the nurses, Hilary hobbled up and down the hospital's hallways, peering into the rooms and wards, hoping to find her friends. After several weeks of searching each room and each new arrival, she had only found two: Katherine, known as Katie, and the other Katherine, known as Kat. They had been injured more severely but were expected to make full recoveries as well.

The hospital meals were small, but Hilary especially enjoyed the days when mushy peas and mince on toast were served and time spent giggling with her friends despite the trauma they all had endured during the orphanage bombing. Laughter had a healing effect on them all.

One morning, as Hilary finished her breakfast in the dining hall, she looked across the table to her friend Katie, whose face was mashed against the windowpane. Several months prior to their arrival, a wayward German bomb had landed and exploded on Giltspur Street. The resulting concussion had blown out all the windows on that side of the building. The last of the windows were finally being replaced.

Hilary smirked at the girl before her and the squished expression on her face before returning to her breakfast.

"Disgusting," Hilary mumbled to herself as she dropped the oatmeal-caked spoon back into her bowl.

"Shut up," Katie replied, her smooshed lips still pressed against the glass.

"What?"

"Shut up, you," Katie repeated, turning her head back to Hilary and looking quite cross.

"I was talking about the oatmeal."

"Oh," Katie replied. "It's not oatmeal. It's parasitic gruel."

Hilary rolled her eyes.

"Be nice, Hils, or I'll make up a word just foh you," Katie warned with bulging eyes.

"Parasitic gruel? You know, I've noticed that most of your special words, your Katie-isms, are interchangeable," Hilary said with a raised eyebrow and a smirk.

"Depends on me mood, it does," Katie replied with a sly grin, turning her eyes back to the workmen.

Katie, who was also twelve, had straight ginger-brown hair, brown eyes, and a freckled complexion. She lost both her parents in a motorcar accident a year and a half prior. Katie found herself at Saint Austin's, suddenly orphaned at the age of ten.

She was known as the entertainer at Saint Austin's and would often break out in song or silly character voices to amuse anyone willing to turn an ear. Katie often would sneak onto the hospital floors via the stairwell and try to raise the spirits of the injured soldiers with a song or a bit of comedy. Katie received appreciative smiles from them before being pinched by the ear and taken back to the children's ward by a nurse or nun who had no sense of humour at all.

"Well, iz time foh me to go to work," Katie said with a false and overly dramatic sigh.

Hilary folded her hands in front of her and leaned forward, resting her chin on her thumbs, her eyes fixed on Katie.

"You don't have a job. You're twelve. You're going to get in trouble again," Hilary warned.

"Nonsense! Shut it. There's a soldier who lost his leg at Hill End. I'm off to cheer 'im!" Katie proclaimed with a grin. She stood, curtsied, and hobbled off.

Hilary smiled as she watched her friend stop at the doorway, take a bow, and begin walking backwards down the corridor. As Katie turned again, her dressing gown opened slightly, revealing her still-bruised side and ribs. It had taken nearly fifty stitches to sew Katie back together after the metal shrapnel which had inserted itself into her side was removed. Hilary was very proud of her friend's courage and compassion.

Chapter Eight

Mina's New Clothes

THERESA TRIED TO force a smile as she handed the precious pile of clothing and boots to Mina, who had been wearing only oversized shirts and huge socks that flapped with every step she took since her arrival but managed only a pained grimace. Melody had urged her to the point of a heated argument to share the old clothes with the foundling. But the thought of Mina, whom she barely knew, wearing *these* clothes made Theresa feel ill inside. They were the few remaining treasures from a life she was trying so hard to forget. Mina wearing them seemed inappropriate and a violation to her sacred memories and would be a constant, painful reminder every time she saw them on her. Theresa felt anger toward Mina as well, though she knew in her heart that her anger was displaced. She stood silent and stone-faced as the child's eyes grew wide and a bright smile filled her face as she gleefully accepted them.

"You need some proper clothes to wear. Theresa had these and thought you might be able to fit into them. Do you like them?"

"Oh, very much! Thank you, miss. Thank you so very much. Thank you both. They are lovely. Yellow and brown and black are some of my favourite colours… and trousers! I've never had trousers before!" Mina pressed her nose to the clothes and breathed deeply. "They even smell like me!"

Theresa's face twitched and contorted at the child's words.

Mina hugged the statuesque Theresa and then Melody, who knelt down and reciprocated with one of her own and a smile.

"I'm going to try on me new stitches! Back in a tick!" With that, she turned and hobbled back into the bedroom to change. Theresa turned her cold eyes to Melody. After a long, silent moment, she headed for the back door, gathering her flute, old pipe, tobacco pouch, and lighter, the screen door slamming behind her.

"What do you think, miss? Trousers!" Mina said, her bright smile beaming as she modelled her new clothes, spinning in a circle.

"They fit you perfectly, Mina," Melody replied. "They look like they were made for you!"

"Where's Treena? I want to show her too!"

"Um… Theresa stepped out for a minute. I don't think she's feeling very well at the moment. Why don't you let her rest? I'm sure she'll be fine in a bit. You can show her then."

Melody approached Theresa as she sat on an old log in the grassy field behind their home. This is where Theresa always came when the stress of life became too much for her to deal with. As usual, she was playing the old tune on her American Indian flute. Somehow it calmed the storm that was raging within her. She kept starting, stopping, and starting again as she grasped for the rest of the song that so haunted her. Only fragments of it remained in Theresa's mind, but every day, many times a day, she searched her mind for the remainder of the song, never able to fully grasp it.

"I brought you a cup of tea," Melody said with a smile as she sat down, setting the cup between them. Theresa continued playing the old tune without a word. Melody sat with her in silence, watching a rabbit search for a meal before she spoke.

"Do you remember when you found that litter of baby cottontails after their mama was run over by a car? You took them home and used a doll's bottle to feed them milk with a little Karo syrup in it, every two hours. You scarcely slept for weeks; you saved their lives. I remember how you cried when you had to set them free."

Theresa stopped playing her flute and stared at Melody for a moment. "I hid them in the root cellar so Thomas wouldn't find them and make me cook them up."

Melody laughed. "I forgot about that. Do you remember when Millie's son took a fall on his bike right in front of your house and you carried him all the way to the pub so that Millie could take care of him?"

"Yeah, I remember."

"He was what, eight years old?"

"Seven."

"And weighed what, about a hundred and twenty pounds?"

"More like a hundred and sixty." Theresa chuckled.

"Do you remember how you cared for Mr Wallace when he—?"

"Mel, where are you going?" Theresa said, a squint of suspicion in her eyes.

"The Theresa I know would have done anything to help someone in need, without reservation, even give the shirt off her back to help a needy child."

"And look where that got me," she retorted. "Maybe I'm not that person anymore."

"Well, that's your choice then, isn't it?"

"Choice? Are you saying I chose this? How dare you!"

"You misunderstand. I didn't say you've chosen all the things that have happened to you. I'm saying it's your choice in how you have responded to them. You've built an impenetrable castle around yourself for protection, without windows or doors, complete with a moat and snapping alligators. No one gets in. No one can get out, including you. You're alone in your own personal hell. *That* is the choice you've made."

Theresa stared at her for a long moment and resumed playing her flute. Melody looked down at the cup of tea between them.

"I'm not sure which has grown colder, you or this cup of tea."

With that, Melody rose and trudged back to the house without looking back.

9 Chapter Nine

Stitches and Lemon Juice

HILARY OPENED THE door ever so slightly, revealing a single eye. "Well?" she said softly as the eye flitted about in fear.

"Got them," the voice on the other side said nervously.

"Well, get the 'ell in here!" Katie called out as Hilary opened the door for Kat and just as quickly closed it behind her.

"For the record, I still think this is a bad idea," Kat warned, her stomach feeling a bit queasy.

"For the record, I think you're a *broken* record, Kat! Shut it," Katie snapped.

Hilary scowled at Katie, who sat on her bed with her hospital gown partly open, revealing her much improved side, less the furious-looking sutures.

"Be nice! She took a significant risk getting these for us. Show some appreciation, won't you?"

"You're right. Sorry. Can we just geh'on wif it?" Katie pleaded.

Kat reached into her dress pockets and pulled out a pair of needle-nose pliers, a tiny pair of scissors, a handful of cotton balls, and a small container of liquid.

"Did you sterilise them?" Hilary asked.

"I couldn't get any iodine," Kat said apologetically.

"It's a hospital. How could you not find any iodine? It's a hospital." Katie said in disbelief.

"They were very busy where the supplies are kept, new soldiers and all. So I improvised."

"You *improvised?*" Katie said, looking quite irritated. "I don' wanna know. Hils, jus' do it!"

"You did well, Kat," Hilary said. "Now your job will be to snip each suture, and I'll use the pliers to pull them out. Okay?"

A look of horror filled Kat's face. Kat, thirteen and somewhat portly, preferred spending her time curled up in a comfy chair with a book or in the kitchen, watching and chatting with the staff about recipes. Kat had been at Saint Austin's from the time she was born, having never known her parents or why she was without a family. She reminded everyone of a rather plump version of Little Orphan Annie, with her fuzzy ginger hair and pale blue eyes.

"I... I don't... I don't think I can do it," she said, feeling another wave of nausea.

"Kat," Hilary said, "Katie's sutures should have come out weeks ago. The staff has been too busy with all the wounded coming in to have time to do it. Look at Katie's side. The sutures are festering. They need to come out now, and you're going to help me, okay?"

Kat winced as she nodded reluctantly.

"Good girl," Hilary said with a smile, taking the cotton balls and sterilising liquid from Kat's trembling hands.

Hilary dowsed the tools and then the cottons with the liquid and began wiping down Katie's wounds.

After a moment, Katie sprang to her feet in a screeching panic.

"WHA' THE HELL IS THAT?"

Kat's eyes flickered back and forth between Hilary and Katie for a long moment as though she were watching a Ping-Pong tournament before she answered, "Lemon juice. I told you I had to improvise. I nicked it from the kitchen."

They watched Katie dance around for a moment as though she had just caught fire, but eventually she settled back onto the bed, ready for the girls to put her out of her misery.

"Do it," Katie demanded in a weak voice.

Hilary handed the tiny scissors back to Kat. She slowly approached the furious sutures that seemed to dare her to cut them. With a loud gulp and shaking hands, she snipped the first stitch—no explosions, no shrieks of pain—nothing. Kat breathed a sigh of relief.

"You're not defusing a bomb, Kat. Get on wif it, eh?" Katie said sarcastically.

Hilary grasped the knotted end of the suture and gave it a tug; it slipped right out.

"What on earth do you think you're doing?" a shrill voice rang out behind them. The girls turned in horror toward the sound; it was Medlock.

"Oh, shit on a stick," Katie blurted out, looking for a place to hide. Hilary and Kat let out a scream. Medlock had grasped them both by the ears.

"Oi! That's enough!" a deep voice boomed out behind them. Medlock released her grip, and the three of them turned to see Old Man Turly looming above them.

"Do you see what they are doing, Mr Turly?" Medlock said defensively.

"Yes, I do! Do you see *why* they are doing it?"

Medlock moved closer to inspect Katie's side. She placed her fingers on the swollen red tissue. It felt hard and dry, almost leathery. Her expression changed dramatically.

"Why haven't they done anything about this? Infection has set in!" she responded.

Hilary stepped in front of Medlock, her eyes boring deep into the old woman, still rubbing her bright pink ear.

"Because the staff is overwhelmed with all the wounded troops coming in. Katie's sutures were supposed to come out almost two weeks ago. They haven't got the time or the staff to deal with these things. We're not a priority right now. Saving the lives of those brave soldiers is! We can handle this, Miss Medlock." Hilary stopped a breath short, fearing she may have already said too much.

Medlock stood silent for a long moment, staring at Katie's side.

"Are these tools sterilised?"

"As much as they could be, Miss Medlock," Hilary said with a mature and confident voice, a voice she didn't know she had within her.

Medlock nodded. "Very well then. Stand aside, Miss May. I'll take care of this, but I'll need your assistance please."

The three young girls in harmony released a great sigh of relief.

Medlock knelt next to Katie's bed and gently put pressure on several of the festering sutures. Balls of pus emerged from them as Katie's eyes bulged in obvious discomfort.

"May I be dismissed, Miss Medlock?" Kat inquired, a quiver in her voice and a look of revulsion on her face.

"No, Miss Jones, you may not. I have some news that concerns the three of you," she replied as she snipped the sutures. "Miss May, if you would be so kind as to bring me the bowl on that tray near the foot of the bed."

Hilary complied.

"We will put the sutures in this bowl. Your job will be to wipe down each of Katie's wounds with the cotton balls and astringent—and do use a bit of pressure as it will help it soak in and sterilise the infected areas."

Katie's eyes bloated, and her head and face twitched and contorted into impossible positions and expressions as Hilary carefully wiped the pus from each small hole with the lemon-juice-saturated cotton balls. Even though Katie refused to utter a single sound, Hilary knew that a powerful string of profanity was running through Katie's mind that, if unleashed, would melt the paint from the window frames and perhaps tear a hole in the very fabric of time and space itself.

"You're being very brave, Miss Katie," Turly chimed in from the back of the room.

"Mr Turly, if you don't mind me asking, what happened to Mina? Did she make it out okay? She's been on my mind," Hilary asked.

Before Turly answered, Medlock inserted herself. "Mina didn't make it, Miss May. I'm sorry."

Turly hung his head and closed his eyes.

"Now," Medlock said as she continued working on Katie, her hands surprisingly steady for her age, "as you all know, Saint Austin's is no more. In order to find a place for each of you, I have arranged for you to be sent to Cardiff, to three different work farms, until this dreadful war has ended. This coming Sunday, Mr Turly will escort each of you to your new homes. There, all done!" she said with smug satisfaction as she dropped the tools into the container.

Katie collapsed onto her bed, her face beet red, and began hyperventilating and twitching, as though she were having a dreadful seizure.

Medlock sniffed the air and stood. "I smell lemon." With that, she turned and walked to the doorway without looking back. "Best of luck to the three of you. Expect Mr Turly just after breakfast. Good day."

10 Chapter Ten

Escape from Bart's

THE THREE GIRLS sat properly gob-struck for nearly five minutes. Finally, when the silence became too much to bear, Hilary spoke.

"Unacceptable," she proclaimed in her very proper and posh accent. "We will not allow that dreadful woman to separate us and send us to... *Cardiff!* Kat, isn't Miss Hatchet working in the hospital kitchen now?"

Kat nodded. "She works the morning prep shift."

"Your job will be to keep Miss Hatchet occupied whilst I gather food from the pantry and clothing supplies to take with us. Katie, you'll need to create a distraction."

Katie scrunched her face, appearing deep in thought. After a moment, she began laughing. Tapping Hilary on the shoulder with her fingers as though playing a wild improvisational piano piece, she responded. "Oh... Oh, I've got an idea! Oh, this'll be brilliant! Leave it to me, Hils! I've got an idea!"

Kat began her assigned mission the following morning. It took a bit of encouragement from Hilary and a not-so-gentle shove in the back for

Kat to enter the kitchen as Hilary's small face peered around the corner at her. Kat stood silent and motionless for a long moment, her intense blue eyes flickering about the room nervously.

"You all right, love? That head injury still messing with your noodle?" Miss Hatchet asked with a smile.

Kat looked back at Hilary, whose eyes were now bulging in anger. "Yes, yes, that must be it. I'm fine. Um… I noticed you're making bangers and mash. So… um… what's your secret for making, um… bangers and mash, Miss Hatchet?"

Miss Hatchet, a very well-fed and underappreciated woman, smiled at Kat, appearing quite pleased to have this young girl taking an interest in her most secret recipes.

Hilary crept into the food pantry and walk-in refrigerator whilst Kat kept the woman talking. It was very cold, but Hilary was on a mission. She had secured two pillowcases from the laundry and began filling them with every morsel of food that could be carried and stay fresh for several days.

Hilary listened to the conversation in the other room for fear the woman, who Katie once rudely remarked reminded her of an overstuffed sofa with a head propped atop it, might suddenly waddle into the room.

"You want to know my secret?" Hilary heard Miss Hatchet say to Kat.

She froze in place; she had to know. Miss Hatchet made the best bangers and mash she had ever had.

"The secret is you taste everything!" she proclaimed.

"But it's raw meat. You don't taste the raw meat, do you?" Kat sounded horrified.

"No, no!" the woman said with a jolly laugh. "After I season it and add just enough breadcrumbs, I fry a bit of it in a skillet with lard. I fine-tune it from there. Sometimes it takes a lot of tasting to get it just right!"

Hilary let out a giggle and covered her mouth, hoping she'd not been heard.

She had nearly filled the last bag when she noticed some glass containers on the top shelf. She climbed up, her fingers sticking to the frost-covered metal, and gasped in delight at what she saw.

"Mushy peas!" Hilary exclaimed in a loud whisper. "Mushy peas! Who'd want to escape when they have mushy peas?" A wide-eyed smile covered her face as she carefully set the large jar into the pillowcase and climbed down. Hilary knew it would be a nightmare to carry, but she didn't care. Her bright eyes danced as she grinned from ear to ear.

Hilary shivered as she quietly closed the latch upon exiting the huge fridge. She found several loaves of hard bread and powdered porridge mix on her way out and hoped that they would soothe Katie and Kat's sure-to-come anger about the large, heavy container. Feeling quite proud of herself, Hilary dragged the full pillowcases out of the kitchen as the contents clinked, clanked, and clunked with every step.

Katie, meanwhile, quietly slipped a screwdriver between the door latch and doorknob of the PA room. She had always been fascinated by radios and sound systems and dreamed of one day running the sound equipment, which almost seemed like magic, at a radio station. Even as a little girl, she was totally captivated by the sound coming through those magical boxes and speaker things.

She often would get into trouble at Saint Austin's for taking apart the radios and pulling all the tubes out of them. She would line them up in order of size next to each other and then call in the staff to show off her skill. She always put them back in their proper slots but was scolded for her pranks and left to run through her beads until her fingertips were tender and pink. Sometimes she even experienced Medlock's wooden paddle, something she vowed to avoid but continually failed at.

The door popped open with a *click*. Katie looked about to see if anyone had heard the sound; it was quiet, no one in sight. She slipped in and lit the candle she had appropriated from the chapel, locking the door behind her.

The system looked complicated with all its switches, dials, and knobs. The big metal microphone, with its strange slats covering porous cloth, looked menacing as she began unscrewing wires from the back of the big box and moved them to different positions. Even though she had never seen such a complicated piece of sound equipment, with all its wires and glass tubes, she knew exactly what to do.

"Where is she?" Kat whispered to Hilary as they huddled out of sight near the boiler tanks in the power room. It was dark, and Kat was anxious. She seemed fixated on a flashing red light suspended from the ceiling above her. Hilary, with wide eyes, studied the equipment in the room, ignoring Kat.

"Hils?" Kat whispered to Hilary.

"She'll be along… and stop looking at the blinking light. You know better," Hilary responded, her eyes still exploring the junction boxes, the gigantic boilers, machinery, and wires.

This room powers the entire *hospital?* she wondered to herself.

She wished for a moment that she could stay here and learn all about the power system, how it worked, what all these strange-looking things did, and what they would do when the power went out.

After several long moments of rewiring the PA system, Katie connected the stripped wires from the power switch she had disabled. She tucked them back inside the metal box and replaced it on the shelf. She crossed herself, let out a deep sigh, muttered, "Greib…" and inserted the plug into the wall.

The glass tubes began glowing one by one, first faintly and then, after a moment, brightly. She lifted the heavy microphone with both hands and blew out her candle.

A horrible squeal of feedback sounded throughout the entire hospital over the PA speakers. After a few taps on the microphone, Katie's voice came over the system. She introduced herself, then began singing a droning and out-of-key version of "I'll Take You Home Again, Kathleen" at the top of her lungs.

The maintenance staff, who were working near Hilary and Kat's planned exit route, rushed from the power room to assist in the capture of the singing troublemaker. The coast was now clear.

"Brilliant. This should take care of the soldiers standing watch outside as well," Hilary said. "Time to go."

Hilary and Kat crept over and climbed several wooden steps along the back wall to a small blackened door and opened it. Cold air rushed through the old coal door from the outside.

"What about Katie?" Kat demanded, following Hilary up the wooden steps, wiping coal dust from her hands whilst dragging their heavy pillowcases behind. The door slammed shut, raising a cloud of dust.

There was chaos throughout the hospital. The screeching song blasted so loudly that everyone covered their ears as the torturous rendition seemed to go on forever.

The maintenance crew and security arrived at the PA room, but the door was locked from the inside. They began banging on it and shouting after realising that chewing gum had been squished into the lock hole and the key would no longer turn the lock. One man chucked a small dustbin through the frosted-glass portion of the door. Reaching through the opening, he unlocked it from the inside. They rushed in; the room was empty. The microphone was missing as well. They tried switching off the power, even pulling the power cord, but Katie had been very thorough in her work; the comm system stayed on.

Katie was no longer singing, but now a very loud ukulele screeched through the PA system, causing the speakers to vibrate, some falling off the walls, frightening patients and staff alike.

The hospital security and maintenance men ran up and down the corridors, stumbling into each other in a frantic attempt to find the source of the sound, unsure if it was some unorthodox attack by the Germans or just a cheeky prankster.

From the rear of the sound system, they began tracing the speaker wires back out the door and down the long corridor. Katie had set up several diversions with dummy wires that led the men in circles to dead ends.

Nearly forty minutes had passed. Eventually the men traced the live wires to the women's loo, all the while to the sound of the ear-piercing ukulele. Charging in without knocking, they found the wires leading out a small window. The microphone sat on the ground. Next to it was a gramophone; the ukulele song was now skipping, playing the same line over and over. A red-faced guard pulled the needle off the vinyl record, causing a horrible screeching sound that hurt even his old ears. He looked at it; it was an old George Formby record. In anger, he smacked it against the window frame, shattering it into dozens of pieces. He looked about the hospital grounds from the open window. No trace of the culprit.

Chapter Eleven

Woods Elves and Mermaids

A YOUNG MAN *stood at the edge of the rocky shoreline at dusk, dressed in clothing that resembled something a noble would have worn from a time long ago in a land long forgotten. The ocean breeze tussled his long blond hair, revealing his pointed ears. He was a woods elf, far from home.*

He leapt from rock to rock, moving farther out toward the sea, the water ever deepening as he was drawn to the siren song. Despite knowing his impending fate, his mind had succumbed to the sound of her voice, and he hurried willingly to the edge of the rock. At long last, he saw the woman who had been calling to him for so many years. He lost his breath as he gazed upon her long, wavy auburn hair that covered her shoulders and breasts and her milky-white skin that was flawless and seemed to glow in the moonlight. He had never imagined such beauty.

From her mouth came a song like no other. The song and words permeated his mind and heart with clarity despite the sound of the ocean crashing upon the nearby rocks. With total abandon, he fell forward into her arms, and they descended into the depths of the black ocean.

"So did he die?" Theresa asked as Mina recounted the story.

"The siren had to make love to him in haste as he only had a few moments left to live. Otherwise, she wouldn't have got what she needed," Mina explained.

"What... did she need?" Theresa asked.

Mina hesitated. "His seed."

Theresa's eyes bloated, a look of shock covering her face.

"Why... why did she need his seed?"

"Um... it's kinda hard to explain. Um... there... there are no mermen; there never have been. All mer are female. If a male is born, it's kind of an abomination, a horribly ugly, sterile, and stupid bottom-feeder. The only way mer can make more mer are with land walkers, human males, and—well, like I said, it's hard to explain."

"Mina, who... How do you know all this? Did your parents tell you this story?"

"My parents *are* the story. My dad was the woods elf, and my mum is the mer... I am the child born from the story."

Theresa sat stunned. She could not believe what she was hearing from this uneducated, simple girl. Had she heard this story elsewhere, or had her fertile mind created it?

Mina sat in her oversized nightgown, which hung on her like a tent, at the kitchen table as she and Theresa had a final cup of tea before bed, her feet wiggling in the air back and forth as they were too short to reach the floor.

"So what do the mer do for companionship? I mean, if they end up drowning their mates, don't they get lonely?"

"Walkers aren't their mates. They just have what the mer need to make more mer. They do take mates though, but only one for their entire life. If their mate dies, they never take another. That's what happened to Mum's mate."

"So if land walkers aren't their mates, who...?"

"Other mer of course," Mina said with another shrug.

"Of course," Theresa said, her voice dropping off, a look of confusion and disbelief covering her face. She wished Melody was here to hear this odd conversation, one of many, but she had to work late at the local hospital treating soldiers who had arrived from the front lines.

"So um... your mum had a mate, another mer, and something happened to her?"

Mina lowered her eyes and nodded. "When I was little. It was an accident, but Mum blamed me, and that's when she didn't want me anymore. She said I was *bàs aislingeach*."

"*Bàs aislingeach*? That almost sounds Gaelic. What does it mean?"

Mina hesitated. "Death dreamer. She said I dream bad things to happen. She said I'm evil. That I bring death."

Theresa sat silent, not knowing what to say.

Chapter Twelve

Books and Friendship

HILARY AND KAT sat shivering on the rusted and disused railway track as Katie, in her overly dramatic style, grilled and lectured them both.

"Aren't you bovered by this?" Katie demanded of Hilary with her arms flailing wildly. "Of ole the stewpid fings to do!"

Hilary could only see Katie's silhouette as the full moon rose behind her. Her steamed breath was reminiscent of a dragon whose breath of fire could destroy all that displeased it. Her eyes seemed to glow a fiery red. Katie had a nasty habit of letting her accent become very exaggerated when she was cross with someone. When it became this thick, no one could understand her.

"Oi! What were you finking!" she screamed at the shivering Kat, who sat, head upon her knees, surrounded by an empty pillowcase with at least ten hardbound books and several board games which she had appropriated from the recreation room.

"Books!" Katie paused for emphasis. "BOOKS! You brough' books instead of your coat and blanket! What were you finking? Shut up…"

Kat hung her head as Hilary wrapped her own blanket around Kat and sat next to her on the cold railway track.

"Were you able to get it?" Hilary asked Kat.

Kat nodded.

"Shut up! Get whut?" Katie demanded.

Kat fumbled in her skirt pockets. After a moment, she handed the small package to Katie.

"Whut is it?" she said. Suddenly the scent of the package contents filled Katie's nostrils. She pressed her nose against the package, inhaling deeply. A smile spread across her face, and her eyes bloated in delight.

"Coffee?"

"I got it just for you. Should be enough for about a week," Kat said with a nod.

"I'm… I'm sorry, Kat. Thank you," Katie responded.

"That's what friends are for."

Katie seated herself next to Kat, also wrapping her blanket about their shoulders. The lights and sounds of the ongoing air raid continued in the distance as the three friends shivered and snuggled for warmth.

"Did either of you remember to bring bog roll?" Katie asked a few moments later.

Both girls shook their heads.

"Oh dear. Back in a mo," Katie whispered.

Katie returned several minutes later, seeming rather excited. "Good news," she said with a twinkle in her eyes. "I found a place for us to sleep!"

Chapter Thirteen

Unicorns and the Henhouse

*M*INA WATCHED IN *delight as the unicorn danced in the silhouette of the largest moon. From her vantage point, she could see the blue oceans and forested areas of the sphere, which never rose above halfway in the Northern horizon. Mina, dressed in a long, soft white gown, plum-coloured shawl, and a head wreath of delicate purple and pink flowers, smiled in awe as the unicorn danced on the ridge above her.*

The forest was just as she remembered it: white ferns, flowered undergrowth, and thick, dark green moss that looked nearly black in the moonlight.

She could hear faeries flying all about the trees, the sound of their wings reminiscent of dragonflies. Gnomes, who did most of their work at night as the daylight hurt their eyes, rustled in the dense mat of the forest floor, gathering fallen figs and tending to their gardens around their homes.

Woods elves in the distance, were singing their songs. Songs which could melt the hardest of hearts.

The trees rose high above the ground, sharing their ancient, whispered stories within the rustling of their leaves and branches swaying in the breeze. Anyone with a still heart and open mind could hear them if they knew what to listen for, especially in the silence of the ancient sound.

Mina was home. She had been gone for so long and was finally where she belonged. She felt at peace to once again smell, touch, and hear the part of her life called the forest.

A voice called out, "Mina?"

Mina opened her eyes and stood with a jolt. The eggs she had gathered in the porcelain bowl fell onto the ground, three of them cracking.

She had fallen asleep in the henhouse, surrounded by chickens. Theresa, who had just entered, stood over her, looking concerned.

"Mina?" Theresa asked again. "Are you all right? Where were you just now? Daydreaming?"

"I was… I was back home," she muttered as she stooped down to pick up the eggs that had survived the fall onto the hay-covered ground.

As they walked back to the house in silence, Theresa watched Mina with a look of curiosity in her eye.

"So Mina, where *is* your home, really? Are you willing to talk about it now?" Theresa asked. "Your name is rather unusual, and I can't place your accent, though it is familiar to me."

"Balynfirth… and actually, my given name is Minastauriel. Mina for short."

"Minastauriel? That's quite pretty. What's your surname?"

"Surname? It depends on which bay we're from. Mum came from Storr, so I guess I'm Storr too. I think… I'm not sure… I guess I really don't have one." Mina shrugged with a downcast tone.

"Oh? That's… interesting. And where is this Balynfirth?" Theresa asked.

"In Caledonia."

"Caledonia is an ancient name for Scotland."

"Is it?" Mina said with wide eyes.

"Are your people from Scotland?"

"People? No. I'm Aoileach. The clans mostly came from Hibernia," Mina replied.

"Aoileach?"

"That's what the Tuatha and Firbolgs call us. It's not a very nice word."

"Tuatha? Firbolgs? Who are they?"

"Warring clans."

"Are they from Hibernia too? Where is…?"

"It's kinda… thataway." Mina pointed northwest. "The Tuatha and Firbolgs came to our world searching for tin and copper, and they took over. They became kings and bossed us around. Now they've gone to war."

"This sounds… mad, Mina."

"It's in the otherworld, don't you know… the other world," Mina said, sounding frustrated. "We're from a different world, a world of magic and trees and faeries and elves and forest folk and mer too. Now they've declared a purge… of us all! That's our home, don't you know. I've lost my way, and I need to go home."

14 Chapter Fourteen

The Boxcar

WITH A PAINED grimace, Hilary untied her shoelace. She winced, gritting her teeth as she wriggled her foot free and stripped off her soiled and tattered sock; the smell was revolting. She picked off the bits of decaying cloth from the bottom of her foot and gave it a light dusting with her hand. She could only briefly examine it when the lightning outside flashed through the open door of the abandoned boxcar in which they had taken refuge.

Her foot was quite red and swollen around the old suture lines. It had become so painful to walk on Hilary had to fashion herself a walking stick from a bit of broken railway tie. Her hard-soled shoes helped little as well. She let out a sneeze, the hundredth of the day. She shivered.

The old wooden boxcar in which the three girls huddled was draughty and a bit catawampus but offered a break from the heavy rain of the cold December storm. After several more sneezes, Hilary's eye caught Katie's concerned glance.

"It's just a head cold. Nothing more. I'll be fine," Hilary said nasally, trying to sound reassuring as she wiped her nose on her ratty jumper.

"Tha's not very dignified or ladylike for a posh bird like you, is it, Hils?" Katie said with a smirk.

"No, it's not," she replied, feeling disgusted with herself.

Kat let out a whimper as thunder snapped and cracked overhead. Hilary and Katie turned their attention to the increasingly distraught Kat. She sat shivering amongst her dozen or so novels, which were now soaked from the rain dripping into the boxcar.

"It's just thunder, Kat. It'll be okay. Don't be afraid," Hilary said as another clap of thunder sounded, shaking the boxcar and filling it with blinding flashes of lightning.

"Hils!" Kat cried out in terror. Hilary, forgetting her sore foot, rushed over to the quaking Kat.

Kat had suffered a head injury during the bombing of Saint Austin's, which had severely exacerbated her epilepsy. Bright lights and sudden noises could, and often would, trigger grand mal seizures.

Katie joined Hilary at Kat's side, but the seizure had already begun. Kat stiffened and began convulsing as Hilary caught her lurching backward, just preventing her from hitting her head on the wooden floor.

"It's okay, love! You'll be okay. Just relax!" Hilary said, failing to hide her own horror at what was happening. As soon as the seizure had subsided, another round of lightning and thunder would pummel the boxcar, and Kat would stiffen and begin convulsing again. This happened over and over, each convulsion worse than the last.

Hilary held Kat tightly in her arms, rocking her gently.

"I've got you, Kat. Shhh. It's going to be okay. Just relax. You're going to be fine. You're going to be fine."

Katie held Kat's hand and caressed her face as the storm passed off to the east, taking the blinding lightning and ear-splitting thunder with it. After what seemed like hours, Kat's rigid body relaxed, her hand slipping from Katie's grasp.

"Kat?" Hilary said. "Kat?"

The storm had passed, but it left behind a thick and bone-chilling fog. The few who had ventured out of their homes dared not travel more than a few feet in any direction lest they get lost yards from their own front doors.

A portly, middle-aged man worked in his front yard, restacking sandbags around his porch as the rain had flooded his house. He gathered his flat spade and began lobbing water from his mudroom out the front door and onto a nearby hedge. After several vigorous thrusts with his spade, he spotted someone approaching in the fog.

As the figure came into view, the man was taken aback at the condition of the young woman. Her clothes were practically rags, her face and hands covered in dirt and mud.

She stopped and stared at the man for a long moment.

"You all right, love?" the man asked.

"I need that," she replied, pointing to his spade. "I'll return it. I promise." After a long moment and an emotive sigh, he handed the spade to the girl, tears welling up in his eyes.

"What's your name?" he asked.

"Katie."

"Can I help you with this, Katie?"

"No."

She turned and, dragging the spade on the ground, vanished into the fog.

Chapter Fifteen

Talking to the Birds

THE KETTLE BEGAN whistling as Melody stirred the pot of beans on the two-burner stove. She turned off the kettle burner and poured the boiling water into two cups for herself and Theresa. She submerged two tea balls filled with loose black tea into the cups. They sizzled as they met the boiling water.

Theresa sat at the kitchen table with an open container marked TOBACCO and began filling her pipe. As per habit, she looked at the engravings on the wooden pipe and ran her fingers over the strange writing, wondering what they meant.

"I thought we were having chicken tonight, Mel?" Theresa asked as Melody sat down next to her.

"Belina—Mina named her Belina—started laying eggs again. I won't roast an egg-laying chicken," she replied.

Theresa smiled.

"What?" Melody asked, smiling back at her.

"Mina somehow overheard you saying that if the red hen didn't start laying again, you were going to cook her up. She's been moving some of the other hen's eggs to her nest before we could gather them," Theresa replied with a smile.

"Aww, that's cute. I wondered why her eggs were brown now!" Melody said, returning the smile. "We'll wait a bit on having that chicken dinner. We still have beans and should get our coupons tomorrow."

"Well, speaking of Mina," Melody said after finishing her cup, "do you know where she is? Dinner will be in about an hour, and she needs a bath."

"I know where she is," Theresa said, shaking her head. "She's an odd one, she is."

Mr Pims followed Theresa out the back door in search of mice as Theresa headed toward the henhouse.

As she approached the door, Theresa peered inside the dirty window and paused.

Mina was sitting on the bench, talking with two chickens on her lap whilst the others nested.

Theresa froze.

This is odd, very odd… even for her, she thought. Theresa strained her ears to hear what the child was saying through the glass window.

"I'm sorry, Belina, but it's time for me to leave. Treena and Melody have decided that they don't want me, and they're going to send me away forever. I really tried to be good, but they think I'm mental. I'm just in the way, so I'll have to find the old tree by myself and go home." She turned her attention to the other chickens.

"You lot need to remember to share your eggs with Belina so she doesn't get cooked up. Okay? I'm going to miss you all very much."

Theresa entered the henhouse. She stared at Mina, still holding two hens in her arms.

"What's going on?" Theresa asked. Mina said nothing. Theresa seated herself next to Mina. The two hens squawked, flapped their wings, and waddled off, clucking and pecking the hay.

They sat in silence for a moment. Mina stared at the wooden floor covered in straw. Theresa lifted Mina's chin toward her face.

"Mina," Theresa started, "what are you on about? We like you very much. I like you being here."

"You… you think I'm a pet. That's what Melody said. You think I'm a pet, and you think I'm mental."

Theresa gulped. "When did Melody say that, love?"

Mina lowered her eyes. "In a couple of days. She'll say it in a couple of days. She'll also tell you I'm quite ill, and then you won't want me anymore, but I'm not ill… I feel fine."

"Lucy… err… Mina, there is a difference between what *is* real and what we *imagine* to be real. Sometimes I think you have trouble telling the difference. Mina, not everything you think is true. Melody never said that you were my pet. I swear!"

"But she will. I know. I dreamed it."

Theresa sighed, realising the futility of arguing with the child. A few forgotten snippets of Theresa's own childhood flashed before her mind. Compassion filled her heart. In some ways, Mina reminded Theresa of herself.

"Come on," Theresa said as she stood. "Dinner will be ready soon, and you really need a wash! You also have straw and bird dirt on your new trousers and blouse. I've asked you not to do that, haven't I?"

"I'm sorry, miss. Please don't be cross. I'll launder them tonight," Mina said, following Theresa out of the henhouse.

"Mina, did I ever tell you that I'm an orphan too? I grew up in Austin's myself."

"No, you didn't!" Mina stopped suddenly with a look of shock on her face.

"When I was your age, I used to make up wild stories too… very much like the stories you told me about your parents. Honestly, I don't remember anything about my childhood at all. I've sort of blocked it all out, so I made up my own exciting stories and created my own past."

"But I didn't make up—"

"The point I'm trying to make, love, is that I know what you're going through. Spending all your time in the henhouse or staring at the trees, away from people and the real world, isn't going to help you heal inside. You can talk to us. We like you, Mina."

Mina grew silent as they entered the house. She gathered some clean clothes from the small tidy stack by her bed in the living room. She poked her head around the corner of the doorway leading to the kitchen to make certain Theresa and Melody weren't about and then lifted a rag doll from beneath her pillow. Mina smiled and caressed the doll's face, picking out a few burnt bits from its hair and clothes.

"Your name is Judy!" she whispered, giving it another caress and a kiss on the forehead. After carefully tucking the doll beneath her pillow, Mina proceeded to the lavatory and began drawing the water for her bath in silence.

Chapter Sixteen

Haggis

H AGGIS WASN'T HILARY'S favourite thing to eat, but there it was, sitting in a bowl on the wooden table before her. The four chairs that only moments before had been occupied with a family sitting in them were now empty but still warm. The sirens were blaring once again, and the families that had shelters scurried below. Hilary felt shaky as she and Katie had not eaten for several days. The haggis smelled very good at that moment.

The remains of the sheep's stomach that the haggis had been boiled in hung over the dustbin like a deflated balloon, torn asunder and discarded. Next to the haggis was a small wicker basket lined with yellowed linen and filled with cornbread. She felt torn between her moral values and their need to survive.

Katie stood guard outside the house, ready to bark like a guard dog and be a distraction to warn Hilary if the homeowners emerged from their underground shelter prematurely. Hilary bundled up the meal in a dusty potato sack and crept out the back toward the dustbins where Katie was standing guard. Hilary knew little about politics, why her nation was at war, or who this tyrant Hitler was and why he was hell-bent on their destruction, but she knew that if she and Katie didn't eat soon, they would die.

Meal in hand, Hilary slipped out the back door. The two girls crept down the dark alleyway toward the boxcar. Suddenly a whistle sounded. They turned to see a policeman running toward them, nightstick in hand. The girls ran as fast as their legs would carry them, clinging to their precious meal. The back alleyway was dark and hard to negotiate with all the dustbins. Katie was quick on her feet, but Hilary fell behind and the bobbie quickly gained on her. Suddenly Hilary tripped, falling face-first onto the ground, the sack of food sliding on the gravel and stopping at Katie's feet.

"Katie!" Hilary called out as the bobbie grasped her by the collar.

Katie stopped, hesitating back toward Hilary, unsure of what to do. "Sorry, Hils!" she cried out, grasping the sack and turning away, disappearing into the darkness with Hilary's cries echoing behind her in the distance.

Hilary, feeling defeated and abandoned, meekly complied with the policeman who had a firm grasp upon her arm. She staggered weakly toward the paddy wagon when a familiar voice rang out behind her.

"Oi! Rozzer-man! You just gunna leave without me? Tha's just rude!" Katie exclaimed angrily as she tossed the sack of food at his feet.

He unlocked the back of the wagon and ushered the two girls in.

"What's in the bag?" he demanded.

"Food!" Katie said.

The bobbie inspected the contents of the bag and studied the two raggedy girls before him. Sadness filled his eyes.

"You'll thank me for this," he said with a gentle voice, tossing the sack of food to Katie. "Tuck in, you two." He closed and locked the back of the paddy wagon.

17 Chapter Seventeen

Sleeping Mermaid

THERESA SAT WITH a sour look on her face as she tapped out her pipe into the ashtray on the kitchen table. Melody added a few more spices to the soup, took another sample taste, and resumed stirring it. In the background, water could be heard running in the lavatory. Mina was preparing for her bath.

Theresa laid the pipe aside, rolled a cigarette, and lit it. After a deep, contemplative puff, she broke the silence. "I don't know what to think of the child, Mel."

"Why? What happened?"

"She's becoming more and more disconnected from reality. She sits all day, staring at the trees or in the henhouse with the chickens. I overheard her telling them that she was going away because we didn't want her."

"The trees or the chickens?"

"Mel, I'm serious."

A long pause filled the kitchen before Melody responded. "She has been through some tough times. She's feeling very insecure. I think that's to be expected," she said, distracted by her search for something. "Dammit. I think the girl took my salt again. The last time she took a bath, nearly all the salt wound up in her bathwater. Would you go check and see if she has it?"

Theresa popped up and headed toward the loo. She knocked loudly and then opened the door.

"Salt!" Theresa said so the child could hear her.

A small arm reached out from behind the curtain with a nearly empty glass container of salt.

Theresa grabbed the container and left the room, closing the door behind her and mumbling to herself, "What's with the salt?"

As Melody set the table, Theresa headed to the loo to inform Mina that dinner was ready.

"Mina?" Theresa called out as she knocked on the bathroom door. "Dinner's ready! Time to get out of the tub, love!"

There was no response. After knocking several more times, Theresa opened the door.

"Mina?"

Again, no answer.

Theresa opened the curtain and let out a blood-curdling scream. "Mina! Oh my God!"

Mina was facedown in the water; she had sunk to the bottom of the deep cast iron tub. The water was completely motionless.

Melody ran toward the bathroom to find a frantic Theresa pulling the child out of the ice-cold water. Mina let out a startled scream as she was wakened from her deep sleep.

"What do you think you're doing?" Theresa yelled as her own terror turned to anger. "Are you playing some kind of game to try to scare me?"

"I… I fell asleep!" Mina cried out.

Theresa's eyes changed from anger to fear.

"Asleep? Asleep with your face in the water?" Theresa's voice trembled. "You could have drowned, child!" As Theresa wrapped a towel about Mina, she noticed the imprint of what looked like fish scales through her pale skin.

Chapter Eighteen

Melody's Diagnosis

M INA, CLASPING HER doll against her neck, had almost drifted off to sleep in her comfy corner by the wood stove when a sound entered her nearly deaf ears. She couldn't actually hear it, but rather, she *felt* it.

It was an ancient song, a song without words, more of a chant, but very powerful nonetheless. She had heard it before several times in her life. It transcended sound and honoured and awakened the spirit of the trees and harbingers.

Theresa was singing it now on the front porch, at least trying to.

Mina wondered if Theresa knew just how powerful the old song was and what it meant when someone sang it or played it on a wind instrument. She wondered if Theresa was aware of who the old trees were or how even now they were responding to the song. *Perhaps*, she thought, *it's better that Theresa can't remember it.* To have that kind of power could be dangerous.

But it also meant that Theresa didn't know who Mina was; she didn't remember her. With tears running down her cheek, Mina soon drifted off to sleep.

Melody quietly closed the front door behind her so as not to wake the child near the wood-burning stove. It was a balancing act as she was carrying two very hot mugs of cocoa and had a large quilt draped over her arm. She shivered at the sound of the trees rustling around her in what sounded like... whispers.

Theresa was already wrapped in her warm quilt and seated in her rocking chair on the front porch as Melody handed her the steaming hot drinks. The trees grew calm as Theresa stopped singing.

Melody shivered again in the evening chill. Once seated in her chair, she reclaimed her cup of cocoa from Theresa. The sirens had not sounded that night, and for a moment—just a moment—the women forgot their nation was at war.

Melody had worked very late at hospital that day and was unusually quiet.

Theresa broke the silence after several minutes. "I hate to admit it, Mel, but despite all the strangeness of the child, I rather like having Mina here with us. Her being here sort of fills an empty place inside."

Melody remained silent but for the slurping sound she made tasting her cocoa.

"Mel? Did you hear what I said?"

Melody took another sip in silence. After a long moment, she said, "She's not Lucy, Tree."

"I know that!" Theresa retorted, a look of shock spreading across her face.

"Do you? You've slipped several times in the past few weeks and almost called her Lucy. Thank goodness the child's almost deaf... I don't think she'd understand. She's not your pet, to make you feel better about yourself and your loss. She can never be a replacement daughter," Melody said, her eyes fixed downward on the wooden porch.

"Huh-uh. Not buying that... What? You don't like her anymore. You're the one who lectured me about being cold and isolated. So what's changed?"

Melody sat in silence, only moving to take several more sips from her mug as she continued staring downward.

Theresa realised Melody was searching for the right words for whatever she was about to say; she knew Melody all too well. After a moment, Theresa lit her freshly packed pipe and awaited Melody's response.

"I had a conversation with Doctor Constantine today… about Mina. He confirmed my concerns about her… about her health."

"Mina's health? What's wrong with her?" Theresa demanded fearfully.

Melody closed her eyes and let out a long sigh. "Have you noticed those little knots on her fingers?"

Theresa nodded. "I assumed they were injuries from her ordeal."

Melody shook her head. "Rheumatoid arthritis, a very crippling disease." She paused and let out a deep sigh. "There is also evidence of physical abuse on her body. That lump and scar on her forearm? Just by feeling it, I can tell she had a compound fracture there once; the bones were broken in a spiral. The break was so severe that the bones actually broke through the skin. Something tells me she had to set it herself. I'm amazed she can use that arm at all. Numerous other broken bones that were never set or healed properly, old scars and wounds. The child has been abused, severely abused, over a long period of time, and I think it was her mother who did it. You know what that kind of abuse does to a person, don't you?"

Theresa closed her eyes, expelling tears. "Oh my God."

"There's more. She also has a heart condition, probably a small hole in one of the valves. She was most likely born with it. Constantine said she won't live to adulthood. She could have a heart attack at any time."

Theresa set down her pipe, then lit and smoked an entire cigarette before she responded.

"Wait. How could he know that she has a bad heart? He's never examined her. He's never even met her."

"I can hear it through my stethoscope. Constantine just confirmed my diagnosis. She just wasn't put together very well, Tree. I'm sorry."

Theresa knew better than to argue with Melody about medical things. Were it not for the fact that Melody was a woman, she would have been a brilliant doctor, better than most of the doctors she had worked under over the years.

"Is… Is there any treatment?" Theresa pleaded, her voice cracking.

Melody shook her head sadly.

"If she stays with us, we will have to at some point bury her. Could you go through that again?"

"No," Theresa said coldly.

Melody nodded with compassion in her eyes. "I'll make the arrangements."

"Just… just give it a few days."

Melody nodded again.

"Weird," Theresa said after a long moment of silence. "I just remembered. Mina said we were going to have this conversation a few days ago. Like she'd already heard it before."

The women sat lost in their thoughts as their cocoa grew cold.

Chapter Nineteen

Manchester Retrieval

MEDLOCK WALKED STIFFLY down the police station corridor, her sagging skin and hollow cheeks making her face even more prune-like than usual. She stopped at an intersection, unsure of which direction to turn. She arched her back and heard several vertebrae pop back into place. The long drive to Manchester during the night had taken its toll on her. It had been very difficult to navigate the damaged roads in the dark, especially with the light shields attached to her car's headlamps. Whilst hiding her presence from German eyes above, they limited visibility.

Had the full intensity of the headlamps been available, Medlock would have seen and been able to avoid hitting the fallow deer crossing the roadway in the dark and avoid the damage to the bonnet of her car. Under normal circumstances, she would have sent Turly on a mission such as this, but as the new facility they had just acquired needed so much maintenance work to get it up and running properly, Turly simply could not be spared. So Medlock had driven through the night, hoping she would be back at her desk by sunrise.

She was quite surprised by how busy this station was as it was only a quarter of five in the morning. She had expected it to be quiet and that she would be back on her way with the girls within a few minutes.

After a moment, she chose to go left as there were fewer people, especially the undesirable and lowlife types being led in cuffs by bobbies, which made her skin crawl.

Medlock weaved her way through the crowd and down the long corridor with lips pursed, holding her handbag tightly against her chest. She was ready to turn around when she saw the door shingle: DI TYLER.

She paused at the door, took a deep breath, knocked, and then entered the office.

A man greeted her as she entered. "Miss Medlock? Hello. I'm Detective Inspector Sam Tyler. Thank you for coming so promptly."

She nodded and shook the detective's hand.

"We are pretty sure these are the runaways we talked about on the phone."

DI Tyler grabbed the clipboard from his desk. He flipped a couple of pages and, after perusing his notes, began. "We have a Katie Clarkson from a place I can't pronounce and Hilary May from Lincolnshire. We were also taken to the grave of a young woman named Katherine—Kat—Ward. The coroner said there was no sign of foul play. She apparently suffered from severe epilepsy?"

Medlock closed her eyes, nodding sadly. A tear trickled from her eye, travelled down the lines on her face and neck, and vanished behind the collar of her white blouse. "Miss Ward's condition was such we knew it would take her one day. Are the others in good health?"

"Quite thin but recovering. The children could also really use a change of clothes. What they are wearing now are rags," he replied.

"Excellent. I will take them into my custody at once. Thank you, DI Tyler." She turned and strutted toward the door, apparently expecting him to follow.

"Miss Medlock?" DI Tyler said.

Medlock turned her head, looking perturbed.

"First off, it will take about an hour for me to process them into your custody. Sec—"

"That should have been taken care of hours ago, DI Tyler! I don't have time for this kind of incompetence. I expect to be taken to those girls immediately."

DI Tyler smiled politely as he set his clipboard on his desk and tucked his pencil behind his ear. He sauntered toward the old woman, folding his arms before him. He towered over her in silence.

"Let's try this again. First off, it will take about an hour for me to process them into your custody—once you have filled out the paperwork. *That* is proper police procedure. There is also the question of what to do with Miss Ward. Arrangements must be made regarding her. This normally would have taken several hours, but I moved them to the front of the queue, frankly, because I need the room they are in. We had a major bombing here last night, Miss Medlock. Many were killed and many more injured. We are sheltering some of the wounded until we can move them to hospital. I need them out of here. Second, you are very lucky that they are not being charged with trespassing and burglary as you would have had to pay a hefty fine and court costs to have them released to you."

"Burglary? What are they accused of burgling?" she demanded incredulously.

"Food… that's why they weren't charged. The children were starving."

Tyler turned and gathered the clipboard from his desk, and after removing the top two sheets, he handed it to her.

"Now," he continued, "there is a chair right over there that you can use to fill out these release forms, or you can leave. It's up to you," he said, the facade of feigned pleasantry giving way to a look of exhaustion and growing impatience.

"May I trouble you for a biro, Detective Inspector Tyler?" she asked, her voice suddenly cracking and sounding weak.

"Here's a pencil. It will do just fine." He pulled it from his ear and handed it to her.

"One last thing. Katie and Hilary have been through something no one should ever have to go through, especially children. I suspect they will differ greatly from the girls that you remember. They need compassion and understanding, not a rebuke. Am I clear, Miss Medlock?"

"Yes, Detective Inspector. Very clear," she replied in a quivering voice.

Chapter Twenty

The Pilot and the Curse

*K*APITÄN KAPPELHOFF CHECKED *the fuel gauge on the panel before him as it hadn't moved for several hours. He rapped the round window with his middle finger several times, knowing from experience that the gauge was stuck.*

The sleeping needle suddenly awoke and quickly gave Gregor an accurate reading of his true fuel usage; it was time to return to base. He sighed with relief as he was weary and ready to go home. Whilst his Messerschmitt Bf 109 fighter plane was a remarkable war machine, it was limited in its ability to travel beyond London.

Kappelhoff searched the sky for the moon, ignoring his compass. Many of the dials on the board before him weren't working properly, but he wasn't overly concerned as this plane had by far been the luckiest and most reliable machine he had flown in this war. He changed his heading for home and studied the grey surface below him.

"Damned Brits!" he mumbled. "Why does this damp little island have to be so stubborn? They are losing the war, and victory for Germany is within reach. Why won't they simply surrender instead of hiding like plagued rats in the darkness?"

Tonight's run had been a total waste of time. Low-lying fog had prevented him and his entourage from locating and taking out any enemy targets.

His greatest victory in this war to date had been the destruction of an orphanage some three months prior, which German intelligence had determined was, in actuality, the British Army intelligence headquarters. He was, however, still haunted by the face he had seen through his binoculars of a young girl standing under an archway of the building when he and the bombers consummated their attack.

He would never forget that face. The thought of it sent a chill up his neck. Why would a child be at an army facility? Was his intelligence wrong? He wondered how many innocent lives he had taken that night.

As he circled round, he was jarred back into the present moment as enemy fire shredded the tail of his plane.

"Scheiße!" he cried out, scrunching down as small as he could make himself as bullets pelleted his plane with an ear-splitting racket. It seemed to go on forever. Somehow he wasn't hit, but terror quickly filled his soul as he realised he could no longer control the plane. A few moments later, smoke began obscuring what little view he had. The engine had also been hit. It sputtered and spewed oil on his windscreen.

Gregor could see flames at the front of the plane spewing out and licking the now motionless propeller, growing in length and fury as he and his machine plummeted toward the ground below.

He thought of his wife, Mila, and his daughters, Kilara and Anna, back home in Berlin. How he desired to look into Mila's eyes again and hear her tell him that she loved him. Somehow, Gregor thought, seeing and holding her and his daughters would make him feel better about himself and what his life had become. What he had become.

He thought of his elderly mother and how devastated she would be at losing another son in this stupid war. Gregor wondered if God, if there was a God, would see him as a good man or an evil man. He wondered if he would ever be forgiven for the lives he had taken.

As his plane began shaking violently, Gregor sobbed. As the ground rose up to meet him, a small house came into view. A young girl on the front step watched as his plane rocketed toward her and the house. It was the very same girl he had seen at the entrance of the orphanage several months before.

"It's you! Are you Death? Have you come for me?" he cried aloud. The last thing Gregor Kappelhoff saw was the child staring directly into his eyes.

Chapter Twenty One

The Dream Realised

MINA BOLTED UPWARD from her bed, gasping for breath, the terror of the ballistic plane still playing in her mind. Gregor's words—*are you Death?*—rang in her ears over and over, overlapping and echoing as her entire body throbbed with each beat of her heart.

She looked about the dark room, the only movement coming from Mr Pims, who seemed to be searching for some unseen item. Mina wrapped her arms about her knees and lowered her head as she began to sob. She had suffered from these dreams her entire life. Some had called them a gift; she considered them a horrible curse.

After more than a half hour, she settled back to bed. With Judy and the purring Mr Pims snuggled in her arms, she finally fell back to sleep.

Mina awoke to the vibration of footfalls on the kitchen floor. She must have overslept. Theresa was already dressed and rushing about the kitchen with a cup of tea and a pad of paper in hand.

Mina watched her for a moment as she retrieved a pencil from the counter drawer and began scribbling on the pad.

With her blanket wrapped about her and the rag doll close to her heart, Mina quietly entered the room and seated herself at the kitchen table next to Theresa.

"Oh good, you're up! I was just writing you a note. I am off to a job interview and will be back in a bit. The kettle is still hot for tea, and there are some biscuits in the ceramic chicken. You can put some jam on them for brekkie. I need you to clean out the henhouse and tidy up the kitchen a bit, if you don't mind, whilst I'm gone."

Mina smiled and nodded politely. "Anything else I can do, miss?"

Theresa returned the smile. "Whatever you have time for will be just fine, love! Shan't be gone long."

"What kind of job is it?"

"It's a teaching job, maths, like I've always had. The school I taught at before was bombed during Christmas of last year. It's hard to find work right now, so keep your fingers crossed for me, okay, love?"

Mina shared a curious look. "Keep my fingers crossed?"

A rare laugh exited the woman's mouth. "It's like saying good luck!"

"Oh! I see. I hope your luck is very good, and I'll cross my toes too!" Mina said with a smile.

Theresa suddenly stopped, noticing the rag doll Mina was holding.

"Where did you get that?" she asked curtly.

Mina gulped, realising she had forgotten to hide the doll under her pillow.

"I... found her. Her name is Judy."

"How do you know that? Who told you her name? Answer me, Mina!" Theresa demanded, her tone quickly filling with fury. "How do you know that? Did Melody give that to you? Did she?"

A look of horror covered Mina's face. She quickly stumbled down from the chair and began backing away from the woman before her.

"I'm... I'm sorry. Here." Mina offered the doll to Theresa with trembling hands. "She said it wasn't your fault. It wasn't your fault."

"Who said that?" Theresa demanded, coming so close Mina could feel the heat of her anger. "Who said it wasn't my fault? Was it Melody? Did she tell you that? What else did she say? Tell me, Goddammit!"

"The girl... the blond girl. She said it wasn't your fault!"

"*What* blond girl?"

"The one I dream about sometimes. She told me where Judy was. She said I could have her and that it wasn't your fault and that it's okay for you to love me. What does it all mean? And what wasn't your fault?" Mina stammered, her voice cracking.

Theresa snatched the doll from Mina's hand and set it atop the cupboard again.

"Love you?" Theresa said with a sneer. "Don't *ever* touch that again! You understand me? Do you?"

"Yes… yes, miss. I'm so sorry! Please forgive me! Please… please don't hurt me. I promise I'll be good! Please don't hurt me." Mina's voice trembled as she crumpled to the floor.

Theresa closed her eyes and hung her head in silence. After several deep breaths, she slowly walked over, knelt, and placed her hand on the sobbing girl's shoulder. Mina recoiled in fear. At that moment, Theresa realised that this was the first and only time she had touched Mina since the day she found her lying in the street all those months ago, apart from the bathtub incident.

"Mina, please forgive me. Please. I'm so sorry. Give me a chance to make it up to you."

Mina finally raised her red eyes to meet Theresa's, nodding.

Chapter Twenty Two

The Deconstruction of Mina

MINA, THERESA, AND Melody sat quietly at the dinner table, eating the fish and chips that Melody had prepared. The meal was being served quite late as the two women had been involved in a protracted argument and conversation over the rag doll incident earlier that day.

Theresa had hoped for a celebration dinner of her finding a new job, but alas, the school had chosen another candidate from the nearly two hundred applicants for the single position. She sat silently at the table, staring at her untouched food.

Melody scanned the evening newspaper folded next to her plate, one article in particular about two orphan girls from Saint Austin's who were found in Manchester. They had been living in an abandoned train boxcar and were being relocated to a different orphanage, one called Elbry House. The names Katie and Hilary, two girls often spoken of by Mina, caught her eye. She decided to contact the orphanage in the morning.

She knew Theresa would be unhappy with her decision, so needing confirming evidence as to why the child should leave, she prodded Mina.

"So um… Mina," she said, "tell me about your parents. Theresa told me you're from a place a long way from here and that your mother and father aren't quite… human?"

Theresa looked crossly at Melody. "Don't…"

Mina gazed into Melody's eyes for a moment, giving only a flash of eye contact to Theresa before she began. "Mum's name is Lir, and my dad was Omar. I never met him, but I know what he looked like because I took some of Mum's memories whilst she was sleeping, but he died when I was made."

"Took her memories… and that's because she was a mermaid, and he was an elf?" Melody asked.

Mina nodded. "Woods elf…"

"So how did you wind up here, in our world?" Melody asked.

"War. The Firbolgs and Tuatha are at war. The Aoileach were— Oh, what's that expression? Caught in the crossfire? They invaded the forest where we lived and started killing and burning the forest, so they sent me here to protect me."

"These Firbolgs and Tuatha sent you?"

"No… sorry. The Aoileach. The Firbolgs and Tuatha started killing everyone. Then they got the Wasting."

"Wasting?" Melody seemed a bit surprised at all the details in Mina's story.

"It's a disease. Once someone gets it, they become very ill. Some die."

"Sounds like a pandemic of some kind," Melody mumbled aloud to herself, half believing the child.

"What does this wasting do?"

"It kills the women and changes the men."

"How does it kill the women?"

"They kinda pop."

"Pop?"

"Um," Mina said, hesitating for a long moment, her face contorting unpleasantly. "Just before they die, black dust comes out of them. If anyone breathes the dust in, they get sick too."

"Mina, that's horrible," Theresa said with a look of disgust on her face.

"How does it change the men?" Melody asked, trying to get back on topic.

"The men, well, they stop sleeping, and they forget who they are, and they get really mean," Mina said with a shrug.

"Does everyone have this disease in—oh, what did you call it—Aoileach?"

"Balynfirth. Caledonia and Londinium too. Anyone can get it... well, except kids. Kids usually don't get it, and neither do the mer, just the men and married women. That's why the Aoileach don't marry or have children anymore. Once the women get married, they can get sick. Sometimes the men... eat people."

"They eat...?" Melody said, her voice dropping off. A grave look of concern covered her face as she took a deep breath.

"Hold on a mo," Theresa said. "This is a wee bit different than the story you told me in the henhouse. You didn't say anything about a disease."

"You didn't ask," Mina replied curtly.

"You also told me you lived in the ocean and you are a mermaid. Which is it, the ocean or the forest?"

"I was born in the ocean, but Mum didn't want me. I liked it there, but I can't muster a tail and couldn't move in the water very well, and Mum tried to... well... so Malon the faerie—"

Theresa interrupted again with a hint of irritation in her voice. "Malon the faerie?"

"She's a forest faerie who would come by from time to time and visit the mer in the coral cave. She took me to my father's people in the woods. They didn't want me either, so they sent me to Balynfirth."

"A faerie," Melody said flatly.

"After the war started and they turned on the Aoileach, Malon opened the tree and sent me through. She told me that there was one other from our world here and I needed to find her, and when I did, the two of us would be able to make the Wasting go away forever."

"*The tree?* You came here through a tree? Like a magical tree?" Melody asked, blinking several times in disbelief.

"Yes, miss. It's kind of a doorway between the worlds, don't you know."

"How will you stop this wasting, Mina?" Melody asked.

"I don't know. I have this key," she replied, showing them the old silver key around her neck. "But I think it's just for the door on the tree."

"May I see it, Mina?" Theresa asked with a deep sigh, welcoming a moment of silence from the mental blast of information.

The girl lifted the heavy key and its chain from her neck and handed it to Theresa with only a flash of eye contact, still stinging from the morning confrontation. As Melody continued her interrogation of the girl, Theresa studied the key, noticing a small stone set into its bow that resembled a brilliant fire agate. Then it struck her. The circular writing surrounding the fire agate looked familiar... very familiar. She compared the writing on the key to that of her father's pipe, which sat in the sweets bowl at the centre of the table; they were the same. She felt a chill in her neck as she set the key next to her plate and resumed her meal, which was rapidly growing cold.

"So who is this other one? Do you know her?" Melody said.

"It's Treena—I mean Theresa of course."

Theresa nearly choked on her food at Mina's words.

"So you're saying that Theresa is from this Balynfirth place too, and she's an elf?"

"Yes, miss. I mean no, miss. I mean she's from Balynfirth, but she's not woods elf."

The expression on the women's faces was one of confusion and disbelief.

"How do you know Theresa is this other one?" Melody asked with a twinkle in her eye.

"I met her at the harvest dance when she was a little girl and danced with her," Mina replied.

"Oh shit," Theresa mumbled aloud, her food nearly dropping out of her mouth.

"You met Theresa when she was a little girl at a dance in Balynfirth? So you're older than Theresa?"

"Just one of her," she replied.

"Mel, stop! You've made your point! Enough!" Theresa exclaimed.

She had no idea how delusional the child before her was until now. Melody had taken her apart and showed that they were not capable of caring for such an unstable child. But she wasn't quite finished yet.

"So do you have any superpowers, being part mermaid and elf, like the comic book hero Superman?" Melody asked.

"Woods elf. Well... I can share my memories and summon the shadows with the fluty thing, and... and I can sing the siren song like Mum. Sometimes I have dreams when bad things are going to hap—" Mina suddenly stopped and dropped her gaze downward, as though a terrible thought had just invaded her mind. After a moment she continued, "Are those superpowers?"

"Dreams, Mina? Like what dreams? Is something going to happen?" Theresa asked.

She lowered her head again, nodding.

"What's going to happen, Mina?" Theresa asked with a hint of condescension in her voice.

"Tonight... soon," she said, her eyes moving to the old clock hanging on the wall.

"What? What's going to happen tonight?" Theresa demanded.

"An aeroplane is going to hit the house."

"Are we going to die, Mina, when this airplane hits the house?" Melody asked.

Mina looked into her eyes. "Only if you're on the front porch. There will be a fire though, so you'll need lots of water... and Theresa's arm will get hurt."

Theresa closed her eyes, feeling sorrow and compassion for the little girl before her. Melody had made her case. Tomorrow they would summon the authorities to take Mina away and remove this troubled child from their lives forever.

Chapter Twenty Three

The Fearsome Child

THERESA SAT WITH tears welling up in her eyes. She had so wanted for Mina to be a normal child. Perhaps in time, Melody would have warmed to the idea of letting her stay, but after this insane outburst, she knew this would be the last night for the orphan to be here, in her home, in her life.

Mina looked again to the old clock. She stood from the table where they had been talking for nearly an hour.

"It's time," Mina said sadly. "Please stay inside till it's over," she warned, closing the front door behind her.

"Oh my God, Melody, she's lost it. The child is mental!"

Melody nodded. "I'm sorry. I'm so sorry I had to do that, but I think now you realise that this can't continue. We are not equipped to handle this. She needs professional help."

Theresa stood and started toward the door. Melody reached out and grasped her by the hand.

"Let her be. When nothing happens, we'll be able to talk some sense into her," Melody said as Theresa wept silently.

The silence was soon displaced by a sound from outside. Their eyes met as the sound grew louder and higher in pitch. The horrible noise became almost ear-splitting.

"Mina!" Theresa screamed in horror as she bolted toward the door. Suddenly the house shook violently. Several windows imploded as the copper kettles, photos, and the ceramic chicken crashed to the floor.

Theresa and Melody pulled on the front door desperately, but its frame had been damaged and could no longer be opened. In terror, they ran to the back and around the house. A fierce wind arose from the west, nearly blowing both women backward. They shielded their faces from flying branches, small rocks, and debris that seemed determined to slow their attempt to reach the front of the house. The angry sound of the swaying trees was nearly deafening.

They finally reached the front porch, what was left of it. Fire and smoke filled the air. Flames were quickly crawling up the side of the house along the ivy that wrapped the entire north side of its exterior. The front porch had been completely sheared away, with only a few smouldering support beams left in place. Twisted metal from the wreckage creaked and groaned as the fireball on their front lawn charred it black.

"Mina!" Theresa cried out. The child was nowhere to be seen. The fierce wind suddenly stopped.

Theresa and Melody, without thinking, began scooping and tossing buckets of water on the fire from the large barrel that stood next to the house. It was normally only partially full for watering the garden, but fortunately, it was now full to the rim from all the recent rain. *Or,* Theresa wondered, *did Mina fill it in anticipation of an event she knew was going to happen?*

The scene was horrific and surreal. The cockpit of the plane had been ripped from its shell, and its bloodied, unrecognisable pilot lay in a twisted, broken position next to it amidst the burning and contorted metal.

A black-and-yellow haze swallowed the house, making it nearly impossible to see beyond a few yards. Only the scattered fires from the debris and the remains of the burning porch provided any light at all.

The two women continued battling the blaze. After what seemed like hours, the fire was nearly out. *A few more should do the trick!* Theresa thought as Melody handed her another bucket of water. Theresa doused the last of the flames crawling up the side of the house.

Mina emerged from the haze. Both Theresa and Melody felt a terrible chill rush up their spines and fill their hearts. A stony expression covered the child's face. The fire and fury in her eyes made her appear soulless and fearsome.

They watched her as she approached the dying man. Mina stood above the pilot as he lay twitching and writhing in excruciating pain. Small fires burned all around them as the stench of his burning flesh filled their nostrils. Mina stood motionless, studying the man before her. She watched as he gasped for air, his lungs scorched and burnt like paper.

"Du bist der Mann, nicht wahr, Gregor?" Mina said. *"Du hast sie getötet. Du hast sie alle getötet."*

As the women watched, the support beam holding up the remains of the porch suddenly collapsed onto Theresa's shoulder, crushing her to the ground and bursting the front door open.

"Melody!" Theresa cried out.

"Come on! I've gotcha!" Melody said, helping Theresa to her feet and away from the scene.

They turned their eyes back to Mina, still standing before the dying pilot, surrounded in a circle of fire and black-and-yellow haze.

Theresa, holding her arm close to her, covered in soot and water, slowly crept toward Mina. Melody followed. They could now clearly see the bloody, charred, broken body that lay before the child. It twitched horribly and writhed in agony, making terrible gurgling sounds.

"Mina!" Theresa cried out. "Don't look at that! Turn your eyes away! Mina!"

Mina knelt before the man. She closed her eyes for a moment, touching two of her fingers to her own forehead. A moment later, she pressed them to the man's brow.

He suddenly stopped convulsing, and the twisted expression on his face turned to a calm, almost serene smile. He opened his blind eyes and looked straight at Mina.

"Ich… danke dir," he said meekly, spending his last breath. The peaceful expression on his face, however, remained.

"*Ruh dich jetzt aus*, Gregor. *Ruh dich jetzt aus*," Mina whispered.

The women watched as the girl stood and turned, stopping briefly to pick up the meowing Mr Pims, cradling him in her arms. He purred loudly. She strode past them, through the smoky yellow haze and strange moving shadows, looking them both in the eye for a long moment. There was still no emotion on her face.

"Mina?" Theresa said in a quivering voice.

Mr Pims suddenly growled and hissed at Theresa and Melody, whilst still purring.

"What did you do to him, Mina?" Theresa cried out, her voice and body trembling. "What did you do to that man?" she shrieked.

"I showed him what it felt like to be forgiven." Mina turned and walked back inside the house, stroking the purring cat.

24 Chapter Twenty four

Elbry House

THE ORPHANAGE THAT Miss Medlock had taken the girls to was a strange place. It was a combination of an old folk's home and now an orphanage for children. It was called Elbry House. Some of the elderly didn't seem all there, and neither they nor the children quite knew how to relate to each other. It was an odd combination, but the war made it necessary as neither the young nor old seemed to have a place of their own.

Hilary and Katie were delighted to be reunited with several of their friends and broken-hearted to find that many others had died in the bombing, including Danie, someone very dear to them both. Her cockatiel, Bernard, had survived however. Old Man Turly found the injured bird near some broken bricks and nursed him back to health.

Hilary and Katie, dressed in new uniforms and looking washed and refreshed, watched the strange ginger-haired girl across from them at the breakfast table. Jenny was carrying on an odd conversation with herself. The girl had a thick Irish brogue and long hair that was braided into two braids. At the end of each braid, she had rubber-banded some white cloth onto the ends and painted faces on each hair puppet. She held each braid up, the hair puppets facing each other, deep in conversation— deep in argument, actually. The puppets were debating whether the milk she was drinking had gone off. The puppet on her left argued that the milk was so bad that if she drank it, it would mean instant death. The other puppet, in a high falsetto voice, argued that the milk was fine and for the other puppet to stop its whining.

Katie whispered into Hilary's ear, "She's lost it, that one 'as. I fink she's gone funny in the 'ead."

"She wasn't like this before Saint Austin's was hit." Hilary nodded solemnly. "She was fairly normal. War does damage to everyone, even children. It takes something away… innocence."

"Aye, it does." Katie sighed.

"Did you know Mina was her only friend? No one else would talk to her," Hilary said.

"Aye, I did."

"Did you know Mina considered us her best friends?"

"No, I didn't," Katie said with a look of shock on her face. "Who told you that?"

"Turly. You know, I can scarcely think of a single conversation I ever had with her, and yet she thought of me as one of her best friends. Half the time, I couldn't even remember her name."

"Whu's on your mind, Hils?" Katie asked after a long moment.

"I was just… I was just thinking maybe I could be making a bit more of an effort with some of the misfits here. Not only do they not have any families, they don't have anyone at all. Life is hard enough when you have someone, but to not have anyone…" Hilary paused. "Maybe if I had tried a bit harder…"

"This isn't your fault," Katie said, pointing to Jenny. "And what 'appened to Mina wasn't your fault. Nor Kat. You do know that, don't you?"

"I know, but I could have been Mina's friend. She was always so alone, even in death." Hilary could scarcely hold back her tears.

"No. I'm not going to let you go there. I'm not going to let you blame yourself! Shut up!" Katie retorted. After taking a deep breath, she continued in a near whisper, "Listen up. We all have made mistakes, and we all have been through some horrible fings. I'z part of being human.

There are fings that happened to me I've nevah told anyone. Let it go, Hils. Learn from it, then let it go."

"What happened to you? I thought I knew everything about you."

"I… I watched me baby… brovah die. Daniel. I held him in me arms when he passed." Katie's face twitched lightly.

"I'm so sorry. I didn't know you had a brother."

"I don't talk about it."

They watched the ginger girl, who was now shouting loudly and drawing attention to herself from the staff.

"We missed Christmas, you know," Hilary said after a long moment.

"Aye, we did. No Christmas crackahs this year," Katie replied. "Missed me buthday as well."

Chapter Twenty Five

The Siren's Song

MORNING WAS NOW dawning. The fires were out; the police had been and taken the body of the German pilot in a black wagon but were unwilling to take Mina despite Melody's pleadings. They had promised to return later that morning to gather the child into their custody and return her to the orphanage. The women had decided between themselves to keep Mina close until the authorities arrived for fear she would run off before they could return for her.

Theresa's chin began bobbing up and down from exhaustion as she reclined on the sofa, Mina's head resting on a pillow in her lap. The child was sleeping soundly as Theresa struggled to stay awake. She unconsciously stroked Mina's hair and caressed her face. She looked so small and frail, hardly the frightening demon they had experienced the night prior, yet they feared her. *Who is she? What is she?* Theresa had no answers as her eyes slowly closed. In her mind she heard music, calliope music.

Theresa now stood before a merry-go-round as it turned. Bright lights and sounds filled her senses. Children sat on wooden horses, riding up and down, smiling and laughing in delight. A white horse came into view; Lucy was mounted atop it, wearing her yellow blouse and brown trousers, clasping her rag doll against her neck. She shared a huge smile as she waved at her mum with the doll.

"Hi, Mummy!" she called out.

"Hi, baby! Hold on tight!" Theresa said with a smile. She ran her fingers through her light blond hair as her daughter disappeared around the back side of the spinning platform.

Theresa felt an itch on her left cheek. She felt her youthful face with her fingers and noticed a slight bump. She gave it a tug with her fingernails and looked at what she had retrieved; it was a bloody suture. She felt another twinge near the same spot and then another. Running her fingers across her cheek, she now felt numerous other bumps and a strange line forming on her face. She pulled each of the bumps off. They were also sutures. The music had stopped. Everything had changed. The bright colours and lights were now sepia-toned and rather dim. Silence filled her ears except for a bitter wind that chilled her to the bone. She looked up at the carousel as Lucy's wooden horse had just emerged from the back side. The creaking carousel slowed and stopped just before her. Lucy was gone.

"Lucy!" Theresa screamed.

Theresa awoke with a jolt that shook her injured shoulder, causing her to wince in pain. She could feel her heart racing as she regathered her senses. Mina still slept soundly on her lap. She silently wept. Mina's presence had reawakened the horrible dreams that had haunted her for so many years.

Her arm ached to the bone as it hung limply in a homemade sling. Theresa took many deep breaths, trying to calm the storm within. After a moment, she eyed the nearly full ashtray on the coffee table before her, wishing she could light a cigarette, but to do so would waken the child. Her fear of Mina returned.

Melody emerged from the lavatory; a towel wrapped about her hair from her wash. Theresa was looking forward to her turn in the tub. She was still covered in soot and smelled of smoke. It was going to be quite the task to wash her own hair with a damaged shoulder, but she couldn't take the chance of Mina running off if Melody assisted her.

Melody approached Theresa. She saw her own fear of the child reflected in her friend's eyes. She lit a cigarette for Theresa and handed it to her. Theresa smiled and nodded in appreciation; Mel knew her all too well.

Neither woman asked the questions that were on their minds surrounding the events of the night before; Mina's seeming ability to see future events, control nature, and the strange power she had over the German pilot. They watched the clock above the mantle in silence, which seemed to not be moving at all, and hoped that the police would arrive soon to remove the child.

Theresa replayed the bathtub horror in her mind, remembering that this little girl claimed to be part mermaid. Her apparent ability to breathe in the water had convinced her that perhaps she was indeed telling the truth, or at least some of it.

But that would require that she also believe *all* the other stories that Mina had told her, many of them much more difficult to accept.

Melody read an article from the morning newspaper. It was the last head count of those lost in the orphanage bombing all those months ago. The article listed twenty-nine children, including Mina, as deceased. She silently held the paper before Theresa, who skimmed it with raised eyebrows.

"Mina," Melody said with caution in her voice, sounding almost fearful.

Mina opened her eyes and quickly sat up, blinking several times.

"Let's go into the kitchen for a cuppa tea. Okay?"

Mina nodded politely. "Yes, miss."

Mina had just dropped a sugar cube into her cup when Melody spoke again.

"How is it you know German?"

"Who's German?" she replied sleepily.

"Enough. That man last night was a German pilot, and you talked to him in German. Where are you really from, Mina? Are you from Germany?"

A look of shock covered Theresa's face.

Mina, not understanding the energy shift in the room, sat quietly for a moment, not knowing how to respond. "I… I know a lot of tongues. That's the truth!"

"How many, Mina?" Melody demanded.

"All of them," the girl responded innocently.

"You speak every language," Melody responded flatly.

Mina nodded with guilty wide eyes.

Melody pursed her lips whilst nodding repeatedly. "*Está bien... Si entiendes lo que estoy diciendo, puedes comer una galleta del pollo de cerámica.*"

Mina silently left the table, heading directly to the now cracked and chipped ceramic chicken. She opened it and looked back toward the women. "*¿Alguna de ustedes quiere uno?*"

Melody's eyes grew wide.

"*Lleve el recipiente a la mesa. Dale una galleta a Theresa, y tendré dos.*"

Mina promptly carried the heavy container to the table and placed one biscuit before Theresa and two before Melody.

"*¿Quieres un poco de mermelada para tus galletas?*" the girl asked politely.

Melody didn't respond. She simply stared at Mina and turned to Theresa; their eyes met. "Her Spanish is perfect."

Theresa searched her mind for a moment. "Mina, *prends des assiettes... pour éviter les miettes sur la table.*"

"*Voulez-vous les plaques blanches ou les bleues?*" Mina replied.

Theresa looked at Mina in disbelief. "*Les assiettes bleues, s'il te plait.*"

"Okay! *Puis-je avoir marmelade sur le mien?*"

"*Bien sur,*" Theresa replied.

Mina smiled and quickly procured the plates and jam for her biscuit.

Melody silently arose and disappeared into the bedroom. A moment later, she returned with several old pocket translation books. She read several phrases to Mina in Japanese, Russian and Mandarin. Mina responded without hesitation in each language.

"How do you do that?" Melody whispered.

"I guess I can do it cause Mum could do it. She spoke all tongues. All her kind do. This game is fun! That last language sounds funny! Can I try one?" Mina asked with a smile. She looked upward with her eyes as though she were searching for a fun question to ask. The smile quickly faded, and she lowered her eyes to the table as though a sad thought had just intruded into her joy. "*Cén fáth a bhfuil tú ag seoladh ar shiúl mé? An gceapann tú go bhfuil mé go dona? An gceapann tú gur bás mé?*"

Melody looked blankly at her and shrugged. "Um… yes, I like vinegar on my fish and chips?"

Mina smiled politely.

Theresa sat staring at Mina for a moment. "That's not what she said, Mel. She asked, Why are we sending her away and if she's a *bad girl.*"

Mina looked down at the table again, sadness filling her eyes.

"How do *you* know that? I thought you only knew a little French. I've never even heard this language. What is it?"

"I'm… not sure," Theresa said, a look of shock spreading across her face. She wasn't certain what troubled her more at that moment—how Mina knew of their plans to send her back to the orphanage or how she could understand this strange language she had never heard before.

"So, Mina," Melody said after a long silence, "tell me more about this… siren song that your mom could sing. Is that why she speaks every language? To attract a mate?"

"It's, um, it's the way they call land walkers," she replied quietly, noticing that neither woman had answered her question.

Melody raised her eyes without moving her head, her horn-rimmed glasses sliding farther down her nose. "And you can sing it too, in any language?" she asked.

"Yes," she replied. "I learned it when I was a little girl." Mina paused for a moment, deep in thought. "Would you like to hear it?" she asked politely, her eyes fixed on the table.

Melody and Theresa shared a glance and nodded.

Mina closed her eyes, a single tear escaping onto her cheek, and then began. She opened her mouth, and an unrecognisable sound came forth. A moment later, words formed around the sound, with Mina's lips slowly moving but out of sync with the words. The sound seemed to be in their heads rather than from her mouth.

Theresa and Melody's perception changed as the song began. They were no longer in their kitchen. They each stood alone, in their own minds, on the coast of some mysterious ocean shoreline, perched on large boulders as the angry tide crashed upon the rocks. The ocean spray and smell of the brine covered their faces and filled their nostrils.

Gradually the crashing waves gave way to an eerie landscape of wild colours and a glistening, still sea. Below the rocks, a figure emerged from the water. A woman. She seemed to move very slowly. The motion wasn't smooth but rather jerky, almost like watching an old silent film.

Her long auburn hair seemed instantly dry and flowed as if a gentle breeze were caressing it. Her intense blue eyes captured their attention. She opened her mouth, and the hypnotic song began.

And now my charms are all o'erthrown,

And what strength I have's mine own;

Which is most faint; now 'tis true,

I must here be released by you.

But release me from my bands

With the help of your good hands.

Gentle breath of yours my sails

Must fill, or else my project fails,

Which was to please.

Now I want Spirits to enforce, art to enchant;

And my ending is despair,

Unless I be relieved by prayer

Which pierces so that it assaults

Mercy itself and frees all faults.

As you from your crimes would pardon'd be,

Let your indulgence set me free.

Mina stood from the kitchen table, taking one last sip of her tea. She gathered and rehung the silver key from the table onto her neck.

Melody and Theresa sat motionless, fixed in an almost catatonic state. Mina's bottom lip quivered. Her eyes filled with tears as she looked at Theresa. She had so hoped to have found a family who would love her. Mina wept at the reality that she was and always would be alone and unloved.

The sobbing girl touched two fingers to her forehead and then Theresa's brow. Theresa's eyes slowly closed.

Suddenly Theresa found herself in the ocean, able to breathe and swim in its depths, with the strangely familiar words of the song still playing in her mind. Yet she wasn't swimming; someone was holding her. It was Lir,

Mina's mother. Deeper and deeper into the ocean they went, one mile, three miles, four miles, approaching the dark, craggy floor. Tall, lonely mountains below the surface surrounded her in the growing darkness. The oxygen in the water was so thin that she struggled to breathe. Her mother yanked her angrily by her little arm, pulling her shoulder out of the socket. Eventually they reached the ocean floor. Lir lifted a large, heavy flat rock and shoved her daughter beneath it. Theresa felt absolute terror as the weight of the rock crushed down upon her, fracturing her collarbone, forearm, and wrist. The pain was excruciating. She lay there in silence and darkness as the water became still again. Her mother had left her there to die. She felt so alone and abandoned. With her right hand, she slowly began digging the sand beneath her away as she gasped for air through the thick silt. Each time she thought she was nearly free, the heavy rock above her would shift, pinning her down ever deeper into the silt. Eventually, after what must have been hours, she wriggled free and slowly swam upward toward the surface using just her legs, her arm hanging limply at her side, the jagged bones protruding from her flesh as she left a trail of blood in the murky water.

Theresa now found herself walking in a dense, surreal forest. Unbelievable beauty surrounded her, strange colours that she had never seen before, nor could even give a name to. The evening sky had an almost purple tint to it, but it wasn't purple. The leaves on the trees also were a strange colour, almost a glowing magenta, but not magenta. Forest mushrooms and flowers lifted their heads at her approach, revealing almost-human faces. Theresa felt not only a blissful calm at seeing the smiling faces but a strange familiarity with this place.

Unicorns, running in slow motion, seemed to glide through the forest. The ancient trees whispered stories of ages past, and she felt their wisdom fill her very being. She felt one with them, yet so alone.

Mountains and valleys covered in lush green, red, and purple foliage. Insects buzzed about the flowers and plants in joyful delight. She looked up and gasped at the sight of two moons, one of which was so close, so bright, so awe-inspiring, that it took her breath away. The moon seemed to be covered in lush foliage, mountains, and rivers.

Woodland elves played the most incredible music that enchanted her ears. Huge, beautiful birds danced in flight above her. Elves, gnomes, faeries lived in total harmony. This was the surreal *other* world of Mina.

Suddenly the scene changed. The smell of smoke and death filled her lungs. Theresa felt terror and confusion. Everyone was running from some unseen predator. Thousands of long wooden spears and arrows pierced the surrounding ground with strange, whistling sounds. Fire, death, cries heard from the depths of the oceans and land filled her ears.

She was now above the clouds, flying away. A beautiful faerie with bluish hair held her tightly as she desperately tried to locate something below. After a frantic moment of horror and indecision, the faerie suddenly dived toward the ground so fast that Theresa had trouble catching her breath. She was terrified they were going to crash into a tree before them, but they stopped just short of it. The tree was daunting to behold, not just because of its size but because of its obvious age; it was ancient. Theresa could hear it whispering to her even now. It was so old. It was so wise. It had witnessed the rise and fall of many a nation and countless thousands of sunrises and sunsets from a time when the land was much younger. This was the tree Mina had spoken of.

The faerie hurried her to the doorway and bade her to enter after hanging the silver key about her neck. The child sobbed uncontrollably as she stepped through the small doorway. As she looked back, a crude arrow pierced Malon, pinning her to the ground. Theresa hurried through the portal to the other side, weeping and alone.

Now she was at Saint Austin's. Somehow Theresa knew these people: Kat, Hilary, Katie, and Turly. She also recognised Miss Medlock with her cold, ice-blue eyes and pursed, wrinkled lips. She instantly disliked this woman even though she had never met her.

The images of the bombing that crushed Saint Austin's and the endless hours she spent buried, clawing her way out of the debris, blanketed Theresa's mind. She felt every fear and every injury that Mina had experienced. Such pain, such loneliness, such rejection this child had endured.

She experienced the long, agonising walk from London after the bombing, and then Theresa saw herself sweeping the porch, the cigarette dropping from her mouth and nearly lighting the old broom on fire. She saw herself running toward the child as all went black. She felt and experienced everything Mina had in a rapid-fire collage of images and emotions. Then Theresa felt love… the love Mina had for her, the love a daughter has for her mother. This was by far the most frightening experience of them all.

Suddenly Theresa awoke. She was back at the kitchen table, Melody calling her name and shaking her out of her vision.

"She's gone!" Melody announced frantically.

"What?" Theresa said in shock, still trying to wake fully.

"Mina's gone. I woke up from that song—or whatever the hell it was—and she's gone! Not a trace of her! Mina's gone!"

26 Chapter Twenty Six

Seeking Redemption

T HERESA STUMBLED OUT to her car, nearly tripping on her overnight suitcase, wincing in pain from her damaged shoulder. She set the yellow-and-brown case on the gravel and pulled on the old stubborn door handle until it finally surrendered, opening with a jolt. Melody had followed her out, talking nonstop the entire time.

"You've really let that little girl get into your head! She's not right and you know it! You have allowed her to pull you into her twisted fantasy, and now you're putting your own life in danger by going on a wild-goose chase to that town that left you in the street for dead!"

"That's where Elbry House is. I *have* to go there!" Theresa pulled out an old barkless stick from the back seat. She inserted it into the petrol spout and checked the level on the stick. There was enough fuel to get her to her destination and, with the little money she had in her handbag, hopefully enough to get home.

"Hypnosis! I'll wager you she hypnotised us! Think about it. You went to university! You studied psychology! She hypnotised us and planted some kind of story in *your* head, this fantasy she wants you to believe! I'll bet she's a gypsy and learned how to do this trick of hers on the road! She has no home! Never did. Think about her accent. It's unlike anything we have ever heard. She's travelled so much that she never had a dialect from any one place. She's a modern-day gypsy!" Melody said.

Theresa ignored her, giving the suitcase one last shove into the back seat of her car, trying to avoid using her damaged arm. As she slammed the door shut, Melody grasped her hand and stared into her eyes. "Why?" she demanded. "Why are you doing this?"

Theresa looked to the ground as if the answer might be found in the gravel at her feet. After a moment, she murmured, "I wasn't able to help Lucy." She lifted her eyes. "Maybe I can help Mina."

"Is *that* what this is about?" Melody yelled, raising her arms in disbelief. "Lucy's death wasn't your fault! It was an accident! You don't need to seek redemption!"

Theresa stood silent with her normally stoic bottom lip quivering. "Don't I? I could have held her in my arms one more time. I could have told her over and over how much I loved her whilst she was passing, instead of running away." Tears were now flowing down her face.

Melody only rarely saw Theresa cry, and it was always and only regarding her daughter. She softened her tone and gently wiped the tears from her chin.

"Had you stayed there," Melody said softly, "Tom would have killed you, and Lucy would still have died. You did what you *had* to do to survive, and Lucy loved you, Theresa. She loved you as much as any daughter could ever love her mother. Even in death, she knew you loved her. You didn't fail her; that bastard husband of yours did."

Theresa suddenly shook her head from side to side as if trying to shake the emotions and pain away. She headed to the right side of the old car and quickly seated herself behind the wheel, slamming the door.

"What makes you think she's going there?" Melody demanded.

"She's *not* going there!" Theresa started the engine, then held up the old newspaper and its story about the children being moved to Elbry House. "But there are people who might have insight into who she is and where she *is* going!"

Melody's voice again became loud and accusative. "How can you know that? You're shooting in the dark! How could any of those kids have the faintest idea where Mina is going?"

"Mina showed me! I know every one of those people now! I know their names; I know their faces. It's like I know them through her memories. They can help me find her!" Theresa pushed in the clutch and put the gear lever into first. "She shared her memories with me, Mel. Maybe she shared where she was going with someone else."

Melody rolled her eyes. "Are you kidding me? It was a trick! She didn't share any of these memories with me! Just that perverted vision! How come you're so special?" Melody demanded, slamming her hands onto her hips.

Theresa sat silently for a moment. The only sound to be heard was the car's engine pinging every few seconds.

She lifted her gaze to Melody's eyes.

"I'm not special. There's something I didn't tell you. Something that happened yesterday." Tears again welled in Theresa's eyes. "When I saw her holding Judy, I became cross with her... no, furious with her. Mina was terrified. She said a blond girl told her where I hid Judy and that the girl told her it was okay for me to love her. Mel, I laughed at her. I was cruel to her, and I mocked and rejected her plea for love. That's why she ran away. I have to make this right... somehow."

"And you think it was Lucy's ghost that told her that? Did it ever occur to you she was just playing you to avoid being confronted about the doll? Come on, Tree! There are no such things as ghosts!"

"I never told her about Lucy or the doll or the doll's name or my part in Lucy's death. Did you?"

"No, I already told you," Melody said with a sigh. "Not a word."

"Well, there you go. How could she have known all that?"

"I don't know." Melody took a deep breath. "Wait... wait until Friday. That's day after tomorrow. I'm off Friday and Saturday; we'll go together. You don't have to do this alone. I'll go with you."

"It'll be too late then. I have to go now. And the vision is fading. I'm forgetting the faces of the people she showed me."

Melody closed her eyes in resignation. "Just promise me one thing. Promise me you won't go *there*."

"Go where?" Theresa asked sharply.

"You know, Tree... *don't* go there."

"We'll see you soon."

Theresa put her foot on the pedal and the old car lurched forward, leaving a cloud of dust behind.

Melody watched with gritted teeth and her hands on her hips as the car sputtered away. She slowly walked back into the house, kicking the stones at her feet. Mr Pims sat on the windowsill, pawing at Theresa's orchids. Melody frowned. "Down, cat!" she barked out. Mr Pims ignored her. Melody scooped him up and settled him on the ground.

Suddenly Melody stopped. The orchids: all of Theresa's orchids had turned black.

Chapter Twenty Seven

Crossley

THE CANVAS TOP of Theresa's old Crossley was no match for the driving rain. Despite her windows being cranked up all the way, Theresa was soaked to the bone.

Heavy rain had started well over an hour ago, though an occasional snowflake would splat against the windscreen. The worn wiper blade did little to help her see the dark, damaged road. The headlamp shields, designed to keep the prodding eyes of the Germans away, made it even more difficult to see where she was driving. She wished she had an umbrella to protect her from the dripping canvas.

Theresa winced as she reached over to the passenger seat to open a small wooden box. Her shoulder ached. By feeling in the dark, she retrieved one of her cigarettes and slammed it into her mouth. She really didn't want another, but her eyelids were becoming very heavy as she had not slept since the fiery plane ordeal two nights prior.

She cranked the window down ever so slightly, but the rain began soaking her right side almost instantly. She decided to wait and placed the cigarette behind her ear.

Melody's words kept ringing in her head. Was she right? Had Mina lied and simply hypnotised them? Was she just a runaway gypsy, a lowlife?

Mina's siren song kept playing through her mind. It seemed so familiar.

Suddenly Theresa let up on the throttle.

"Shakespeare! The song was from the Tempest! Bloody hell," she said aloud. "She was quoting Shakespeare. That little liar!"

Theresa realised it must be true. Gypsies were well known in the distant past for their Shakespearian plays given to crowds for money whilst pickpockets would rummage through the coats of the mesmerised audiences, looking for valuables.

"It's all a lie," she reasoned aloud. "Being part mermaid and part elf— woods elf," she said mockingly, rolling her eyes. "Being able to breathe underwater. The so-called memories that she shared with me. It's all rubbish! Even what she did to that Nazi. Rubbish! It *must* have been hypnosis. Damn! The child made a fool of me. Bloody 'ell!"

Her car had coasted to a near stop. The sound of the rain pounded the dripping canvas top. For a moment, she considered turning back.

"She lied to us, she lied to *me*! She used and manipulated me!" Theresa said in disappointment and then anger.

Still, she decided to press on to the orphanage. She had to know everything; she had to know the whole truth about Mina.

Chapter Twenty Eight

Settled In

HILARY WATCHED THE snow falling in silence. Being so far north in Scotland, she would have to get used to this scene. It was quite lovely to behold, and she found a peace and serenity in it. It was silent… so very silent. The radio weather forecast predicted that this would turn to rain later that day, so Hilary enjoyed the view whilst she could.

After a moment, she let out a shiver; it was time to go in. She closed the door tightly behind her lest the icy breeze, which was stirring, would catch the door, slam it against the exterior wall, and chill the elderly folk inside.

The new surroundings were taking a bit of getting used to, being blended with a nursing facility and all, but she enjoyed talking with and helping the older folks as they had many wonderful stories to tell, and they enjoyed hearing about her recent adventures as well.

Hilary could hear music as she approached the common room. She peered in the doorway and smiled at the sight of Katie, who was trying to persuade the old folks into a singalong.

Katie had somehow rewired a phonograph so that she could sing through a microphone, and her voice would project out of the hidden speaker inside the cloth box.

"I'll paten' this one day, I will. I'll call it Kaytee-O-Graph!" Katie would say as the elders gaped at her strange machine that you could sing along with.

"You should call it a croaking machine!" one old wag blurted out. "Who'd want that?"

Others would say to themselves or each other, "I'd be too embarrassed to hear my own voice or sing along with Vera Lynn!"

Nonetheless, the old biffers, as Katie referred to them, really seemed to enjoy her talent and social skills, despite struggling to understand her thick accent. The undermanned staff seemed quite content letting her do her shows too; happy residents were less work.

Hilary looked over at Danie's cockatiel, Bernard, who now sat unhappily in a wire cage near the entrance to the common room. At the sight of her, he began chattering, whistling, and running through the phrases that he knew. Mostly he would say, "Where's that cat? Do I look fat in this? Don't eat me! Snarfle glorm, snarfle glorm," and "Here kitty kitty kitty!"

He looked quite dreadful now as he was moulting. *Nothing is sadder-looking than a moulting bird,* Hilary thought.

A commotion near the front entrance captured Hilary's attention; it was Mr. Green again. He loved to park his wheelchair in front of the main entrance and set the chair's brake so that no one could get past him whilst attempting to enter the building.

Mrs Wiggins, a nurse who worked at the home, stopped next to Hilary as the daily scene once again took place.

"He's at it again, cheeky bastard," she said in her thick Manchester accent. "Every day the same thing."

Her arms were folded as she watched two of the staff removing the protesting Mr Green from the doorway.

"Wonder why he does it, eh?" Mrs Wiggins mused aloud.

"Oh, that's easy," Hilary responded. "He likes to watch the nurses come in wearing their work dresses. He fancies their legs."

They watched silently for a moment. Mr Green, with unintelligible grunts, protested removal from his favourite observation spot, then— as the two nurses coming on duty entered—he halted and fixed his eyes upon the chilled women's bare legs.

"Oh my!" Mrs Wiggins exclaimed. "You're quite right! That ole coot!"

She looked to Hilary. "How did you know that, Hils?"

"One time I was trying to talk to him whilst he was staring at the empty fish tank, and one of the nurses walked by. It was the same look. He looked over at me and said, 'You can look, but you can't touch.'"

Mrs Wiggins raised her painted eyebrows. "He talked? Mr Green talked! I've been here four years, and he's never said a word, just mumbles when he gets pulled from the doorway!"

Suddenly a loud *poof!* came from the other room where Katie was entertaining on her hot-wired phonograph. Hilary and Mrs Wiggins hurried in to see what had happened. The room was filling with black smoke. Katie's ingenious machine had exploded, and flames began leaping from the back of the phonograph.

"Fire!" someone cried out. "Fire!"

Chapter Twenty Nine

Icy Roads and Mr Wallace

THERESA STOOD SILENTLY, studying the dark shapes that surrounded her. The scene was monochromatic and surreal, with shades of grey and blackish blue along the moors. She wished she had her camera with her as it was breathtakingly beautiful but doubted that she would have been able to capture this moment with the limitations of film and her hands shaking from the cold. A frozen glaze covered the ground and trees. The snow, mixed with freezing rain, had ended nearly an hour ago, leaving a white blanket in the night sky.

She shivered and put out her cigarette amidst the remnants of the other two she had smoked previously.

Her surroundings looked unspoiled except for the tyre tracks from her car. The skid marks told the story. She looked at the path her wheels had left in the snow. From the roadway, she followed with her eyes to where the car had lost control and slid sideways, ending its journey directly in front of a pine tree. Her car now rested there in silence.

She calmly walked to the front of the car, fearing the worst. *Is the radiator damaged?* she wondered as she stepped gingerly on the slick surface.

To her surprise, just the right wheel rim was bent in a bit. She ran her hand under it to see if there was enough clearance for the tyre to turn; there was. She would have to pound it back into place when she got home. Theresa could already hear all the I-told-you-so's from Melody. She hated when Melody was right, and Theresa was now quite sure that she was.

After a moment, she pressed on. The town was only an hour away. Theresa instinctively knew that, as she used to live there in what seemed to be another life. A horrible, painful life, which oft crept into her dreams at night and tormented her in night terrors.

Thomas, her former husband; Lucy, her deceased daughter; and the townspeople terrified of the rage and soullessness of Tom Collins.

Theresa decided she should sleep a few hours before entering town. It was her dozing off, after all, which had caused the accident that could have killed her a few moments ago. She rubbed her collarbone and felt the welt on her forehead. There was some kind of liquid on it. She looked at her fingers; they were covered in blood. Her head had collided with the steering wheel during the impact with the tree. She was fortunate to be alive.

Old Mr Wallace had a house up the road only a few minutes from here. She would rest there a bit before going into town in the morning.

Theresa turned the starter motor of the car. After a moment, it chugged back to life.

"Good boy." She gave the steering wheel an appreciative pat.

The gearbox ground noisily, disturbing the quiet night as it finally found its way into reverse. The wheels spun a bit, but eventually they found traction in the gravel beneath the snow. The car lurched violently back onto the road. Theresa noticed that the front right headlamp was now out. It was going to be even more difficult to see to drive. Fortunately, the snow and white night sky provided some light of its own. She moved on, anticipating the turn to Wallace's house just up the road.

Her thoughts returned to the past. She remembered her joy as Thomas had brought home one of Wallace's bloodhound pups. She instantly named him Milton.

Thomas was quite cross with her for naming a hunting dog Milton, but as it seemed to be the only name he would respond to, Thomas eventually relented and called him Milton as well.

She also recalled how angry Thomas would become when the dog failed, time after time, to perform in the hunt. Thomas said Milton did it deliberately to make him look the fool.

Then she remembered when Thomas, in a rage, took his hunting rifle and shot Milton between the eyes after yet another failed hunt. He said the dog deserved it as he was such a failure.

When Theresa began crying, Thomas turned the barrel of the rifle toward her, pressing it against her temple, and said with a sneer, "Stop your protest, woman, or you'll be next!"

Theresa approached the old house, her remaining headlamp revealing what had become of it. Her emotions marinated in silence for a long moment, her eyes filling with tears.

Vines and overgrowth now covered the once beautiful stone building. The glorious gardens and landscaping, so meticulously designed by Wallace and his wife, were now compost. Dead weeds and brush were reclaiming the house and land except for a single rosebush that, surprisingly in the dead of winter, had a single white flower in bloom. Theresa imagined that Wallace had somehow left that rose for her. All that remained of his home now was a shell collapsing in on itself from the harsh Scottish winters. It seemed so lonely. Her thoughts revisited her memories of Mr Wallace.

He was a proud Scotsman with a thick brogue. People would come from many miles away to purchase one of his valued pups. He insisted everyone call him Mr Wallace, including his wife, Martha. He thought it to be proper.

His wife had died the summer of '28, and after Martha passed, Mr Wallace's health declined quickly.

Despite Thomas's abusive protests, Theresa cared for Mr Wallace for nearly a month as he grew too weak to care for himself. She bathed and fed him. She read him books—mostly gardening books, which were his favourite—as he would lie in his bed, each day growing weaker.

The day before his passing, Mr Wallace, whispering in Theresa's ear, gave her permission to call him Robert. No one still living knew his first name, and he shared it with her as an ultimate act of love and gratitude.

In the morning, she would drive to town, hopefully unseen, and find out who Mina really was and if Hilary, Katie, and Mr Turly, whom Mina had talked about frequently, were actual people or just another lie. But she had two stops to make first. She tried to get as comfortable as possible, with her woollen blanket wrapped about her. She shivered slightly as she closed her eyes. Music began playing in her mind.

Theresa knelt down, offering Lucy some candy floss. The young girl smiled as she pulled a pink section from the swirl of spun sugar and popped it into her mouth, saving a small piece to offer her doll, which she held tightly against her neck.

"Would you like a bite, Judy? No? Okay, I'll eat it then! You don't know what you're missing!" Lucy said with a laugh.

They walked hand in hand through the carnival, with swarms of faceless people all about them. Theresa smiled down at her daughter as the child seemed so enthralled with all the rides and bright lights.

"Merry-go-round! Can I ride the merry-go-round, Mummy? Please?" Lucy pleaded with wide eyes.

Theresa pinched her eyebrows together for a moment, hesitating at Lucy's request. Something… didn't feel quite right, but Theresa couldn't put her finger on it. After a moment, the feeling faded, and she smiled. "Sure, baby! Go ahead!"

As Theresa sat Lucy upon a white wooden horse, that uncomfortable feeling arose within her again. "Hold on tight, baby!" she warned.

"I will!" Lucy said with a bright smile.

Soon the carousel began turning, with every horse bobbing up and down in an alternating unison. Theresa and Lucy would wave and smile at each other during every rotation of the merry-go-round. As the white horse disappeared around the back of the carousel, the colours faded. A chill ran up Theresa's neck; this felt familiar. Something was wrong.

After a moment, she could see the white horse emerging from the back side. Theresa breathed a sigh of relief. Lucy was still upon it, tightly clutching the brass pole with one hand and her doll with the other. As the horse passed in front of her, Theresa felt the breath leave her body. The child wasn't Lucy; it was Mina. She was wearing the same yellow blouse and brown trousers that Lucy had been wearing just moments before, but a stony expression filled her face. Her eyes seemed to burrow into Theresa's. Soon the horse disappeared around the back side again. When it finally returned, its rider was gone, but the doll remained, lying sideways across the painted wooden saddle. The horse coasted to a stop just in front of Theresa, looking worn and aged. After a moment, the burned and smouldering doll fell to the ground in slow motion, smoke rising from it.

"No!" Theresa screamed, falling to her knees.

She opened her eyes with a start. She was back in her car. All she could see was white. Everything was white! In a panic, she began flailing about her car, pounding on the snow-covered windows, terror filling her soul. With great effort, she cranked the driver's side window down. She plunged her arm deep into the snow surrounding her. Suddenly an avalanche of the heavy white stuff fell inward on her, filling her car and burying her alive.

Theresa opened her eyes; the nightmare was over. Raindrops mixed with snow were silently pelting her windscreen. She took several deep breaths and grasped the steering wheel, resting her head on the back of her trembling hands.

"This has really been a shitty day," she muttered to herself as she slowly regained her composure.

30 Chapter Thirty

Stops Along the Way

THERESA STOOD MOTIONLESS as the snow, flake after flake, covered her shoulders and hair. Her black peacoat now appeared almost white. The ends of her maroon scarf danced in the bitter breeze swirling about her, tiny balls of ice clinging to the end of each tassel. The only sound she could hear was the sound of her own breath, which gathered before her as steam, then vanished into the cold air. Snowflakes clung to her eyelashes as she gazed, unblinking, at the gravestone before her. Her dim eyes didn't seem to reflect any light at all. The grey marbled stone said it all:

LUCY ANNE COLLINS
BORN: 15 January 1920
DIED: 30 October 1929

This was only the second time that Theresa had stood before her daughter's grave, though it had haunted her dreams for years. The first time was in the dead of night, several days after Lucy's funeral, a funeral she couldn't dare attend. Her mind flashed back to that horrible time. She remembered the bitterly cold rain and freezing fog of that night. Her body trembled as Melody helped her through the creaking, rusted iron gates and the menacing, overgrown vines and ravens protesting angrily as they entered the graveyard with only a small torch to light their path. She remembered sobbing in Melody's arms as her friend tried to comfort her, the sutures in her cheek tearing open and her own blood running down her neck and throat. She remembered the horrible sickness she felt inside as the two of them left this godforsaken town for good with only her hope chest and a few mementos to her name, which they had retrieved from her husband's house whilst he was in the pub just moments before.

Movement in the corner of her eye brought her back to the moment. Fear arose in her as she turned. Theresa let out a sigh of relief as a small white rabbit disappeared down a rabbit hole by a nearby gravestone.

Theresa crept toward the grave. Falling to her knees, she brushed the snow from the base of the gravestone and carefully placed the single white rose before it. She placed her hand on the wet ground for a long moment in the exact spot she guessed her daughter's head would be resting beneath the earth, her tears mixing with the snow.

In her mind's eye, she imagined herself lying in the grave with her daughter, holding her child close to her heart, holding Lucy in her arms for eternity in the silent darkness...

"That's how it should have been," she said aloud.

After gently kissing the gravestone, she rose. She looked to the eastern horizon, through the dark, leafless trees. The sun was trying to break through the clouds; it was dawn.

Theresa had one more stop to make, then on to Elbry.

Melody's warning echoed in Theresa's head as she approached the abandoned house: "Don't go *there*..."

She looked about nervously for a long moment before shutting her car engine off.

She lifted the rusted latch to the old iron gate and gave it a push. The bottom of the gate dragged against the concrete walkway and stopped, refusing to yield to her any further. Its stubbornness almost seemed to say *Keep out! You are not welcome here!* Theresa was persistent, however, and managed an opening just wide enough to squeeze through.

She stood motionless for a long moment at the site of her former home. Several storm shutters hung askew, barely attached to the house. The windows and doors were boarded up with weathered and aged plywood. Paint was curled and peeling from the body of the house. It almost seemed angry to see her.

Theresa whipped her head about, certain she had just heard whispers and the sound of a child laughing, but there was no one there. The old rope swing and its wooden seat in the dead oak tree moved to and fro in the breeze. She heard the whispers again and closed her eyes. After a moment, they stopped.

Theresa worked her way around the back of the house, through the overgrown weeds and brush, again hearing the laughter of a child.

"Higher, Mummy!" the girl's voice cried out. Theresa turned toward the sound. The swing was now moving to and fro quickly, far too quickly for what the gentle breeze could have caused. A chill ran up her neck.

As she approached the back entrance, she heard the child crying, "Mummy, I hurt my knee! I hurt my knee!"

Theresa stopped, again closing her eyes, shaking her head and mumbling to herself, "There are no such thing as ghosts."

After a deep breath, she looked about; all was silent again. Theresa tugged on the boards from whence the door once stood. Light revealed the darkened kitchen as she pulled the boards loose, several of them splintering into jagged shards. Dust filtered out of the silent tomb into the morning sunlight. Theresa stooped down and entered the house through the small opening she had made. The kitchen was blackened and smelled of old, burnt wood.

Suddenly ghostly transparent images began moving all about her. She could hear not only the child's voice but that of a woman too.

She watched the young blond woman turning a dial on the gas stove and preparing to light it with a wooden match.

"Mummy!" the girl cried out, hurrying into the kitchen from outside. She ran straight through Theresa to the blond woman, as though Theresa were the ghost.

Theresa felt completely paralysed, unable to even blink as the vision played out before her. Her entire body quivered as though an electrical charge jolted through her, holding her in place. As the young woman spoke, Theresa found herself mumbling the same words in synchronous harmony.

"What's wrong, baby?" both women replied.

"Mummy, I hurt my knee! I fell off the swing and I hurt my knee!" the girl sobbed.

"Oh no. Let's have a look-see, baby. Oh my, that's a nasty scrape!" The woman lifted the child onto the kitchen table and quickly hugged her, showering her with kisses.

"Mummy will fix that up straightaway! It'll be as good as new in no time!" the woman said with a quivering, false smile.

The young girl caressed the woman's face. "It wasn't your fault, Mummy! It wasn't your fault! I'll tell Daddy. I'll tell him I was just clumsy and I fell down! I won't let him hurt you. I promise! It wasn't your fault."

Theresa's face twitched in harmony with the younger version of herself, even down to the eye tic. She felt her knees buckling as she collapsed onto the floor, her eyes still fixated on the apparitions before her.

Whilst the woman cleaned the child's wound with trembling hands and carefully and lovingly covered it with gauze and tape, Lucy looked over to where Theresa sat on the floor. "Look, Mummy! It's you!"

The young woman looked to where Lucy was pointing, her eyebrows pinching together. "It's just a trick of the light. It's the dust swirling in the sunshine."

Theresa felt an icy chill. *Had Lucy just seen her?*

"Let's go to Auntie Melody's now. Don't wait till Daddy goes hunting. Let's get in the car and go now. We can all leave together, and he'll never hurt you again. Please, Mummy?" Lucy pleaded.

Young Theresa smiled at the child and nodded. "Get Judy and we'll go!"

Lucy hurried into the bedroom as the young woman stood in the doorway, placing a cigarette into her mouth.

Theresa looked up at the ghostly version of herself and said in a quivering voice, "Don't light it, Theresa. Don't light the match. Don't! *Don't light the match!*"

The ghost stopped for a moment, looking toward Theresa. She seemed to move in slow motion as she then began scraping a wooden match against the doorframe.

Theresa's eyes flashed toward the gas stove and back to the blond woman in the doorway, then to Lucy, who was just returning from the bedroom, holding her doll and wearing a big smile.

"Nooo!" Theresa screamed.

Suddenly a deafening explosion and blinding light filled her every sense; then an icy darkness enveloped her. As the shadows had stolen the light from the room, she lay mumbling to herself, her body twitching uncontrollably, consumed by the darkness.

"No... No... No... No... No..."

Theresa had nearly drifted off to sleep when the sound of creaking wood entered her ears; someone was walking toward her.

She lifted her eyes as she felt a hand caress her damaged cheek.

"It wasn't your fault, Mum," Lucy said in a gentle voice as she knelt down. "It was an accident. You need to forgive yourself. You hear me? Mum? You need to forgive yourself."

The woman began sobbing. "Baby, I love you so much. I miss you. Lucy, I want to be with you. I want to be with you forever."

"I love you too, Mum, but it's not time yet." The ghost smiled at her mother. "Listen, this is very important. It's okay for you to care about her. It's okay for you to love her. Here, take this," the child said, reaching out her hand toward her mother.

Theresa felt something touch her palm. She looked down and gasped; it was a small heart necklace with an oval garnet birthstone set in the middle. Theresa had given it to Lucy on her ninth birthday.

"Give it to her. Tell her it's from me."

When Theresa looked back up, Lucy was gone.

"Lucy?" Theresa called out frantically. "Lucy!"

She quickly checked her hand again. The necklace was still there. Theresa clutched it tightly as she began sobbing in the darkness, lost in the ruin of herself.

Chapter Thirty One

Mr Fix-it

TAD TURLY WAS most at home in his workshop. He loved to fix things and was quite good at it. Most of his duties surrounded maintaining the buildings and keeping the vehicles running properly.

The years had carved deep lines around his eyes, mouth, and high cheekbones as Tad was well into his seventies. He walked with a cane, from his claim of being wounded in the First World War.

Tad was quite tall but walked hunched over, leading with his huge nose. His snow-white hair stood at end despite his best combing efforts each morning.

He was a man of integrity and always tried to do what was right despite often butting heads with Medlock, who only seemed to care about donations to the orphanage and keeping the children quiet.

Tad peered intently through his thick reading glasses at the phonograph that had caused such a commotion yesterday. He had removed the pegboard back and was examining its inner gubbins for some hidden truth within.

Katie stood quietly, unable to sit down next to him because of her still stinging bum. The headmistress had paddled her with an old wooden board that had numerous holes drilled in it to make sure her point was made.

"Hmm," he said.

"Hmm whuh?" Katie inquired.

"Here is the problem," Tad replied, holding up the power cord. "This cord is worn out. Look how the wires are brittle and frayed."

Katie opened her eyes wide, staring at the charred, cloth-covered electrical cord.

Tad turned to Katie, peering over the top of his glasses. "It wasn't anything you did, Miss Katie; the cord was just worn out. That's what sparked the fire. Would've happened anyway."

"So Medlock paddled me bum for nuffin?" she said, looking irritated.

"Yep," Tad replied. "And she is going to hear about it from me for certain. With a bit of jiggery-pokery and a new, heavy-duty cord, I'll have this as good as new. The Katie-o-graph will rise again!"

Just then Hilary pushed the heavy wood door aside and entered, looking quite excited. "I have news!" she proclaimed, clasping her hands together.

"Whuh iz it, Hils?" Katie asked.

"A woman just arrived," Hilary said. "I was watching Jenny's hair puppets having another row in the common room when I saw a car drive up. At first I thought she just came in to use the loo, 'cause she was in there so long. She came in with blood on her head and her hair mussed about, but when she came out, she was all scrubbed up and headed straight for Medlock's office. I followed her… curiosity…," Hilary said with a shrug. "Anyway, she came to talk about Mina! Mina's alive!"

"Shut up," Katie responded in disbelief.

"Mina? Mina's alive? What does the woman look like, Hilary?" Tad demanded.

"Erm, tallish, old," she replied.

"How old?"

"Fortyish maybe? She has blondish-grey hair. She's pretty, but she has a big scar on her face." Hilary drew a long line on her left cheek to the corner of her mouth with her finger.

"Hmmm." Tad tapped his chin. "I wonder…" With that, he rose to his feet, put on his coat, gathered his cane, and shuffled toward the door.

Katie and Hilary charged out of the old converted livery stable and through the snow toward the main building. Tad followed as quickly as he could, cane in hand, calling out to the girls to come back.

They hesitantly walked back toward Tad, huffing, out of breath from their sprint.

"Why cannae we go?" Katie demanded in a frantic tone.

"Medlock will give you the back of her hand for sure if you go barging in there," Tad replied. "I'll go."

He pulled out his little notepad from his shirt pocket and scribbled on it. He tore the page off, folded it in two, and handed it to Hilary.

"Here," he commanded. "Take this over and put it under the woman's windscreen wiper."

"Oi! Why does she get to carry the note?" Katie protested with ping-pong eyes.

"You don't know what the car looks like!" Hilary retorted.

"Oh yeah, roight then."

"Don't be seen!" Tad warned sternly as the two girls were already racing away.

Tad hurried as quickly as he could toward Medlock's office. He quietly crept to the open doorway, listening intently. He overheard what was becoming a stern lecture by Medlock.

"And you let her leave?" Medlock said in an accusatory tone.

"A German plane crashed on our property. I think it must have frightened her, and that's why she ran away," the woman said, sounding defensive. "Look, Miss Medlock, I just spent nearly the entire night in my car on these icy roads to come up here and talk to you about Mina. All I want is some information about her. I am concerned for her safety."

"I'm sorry, Mrs Collins," Medlock said. "I am not at liberty to give out any information about one of our children, especially to one who didn't have enough sense to ring the authorities about her and then let her run off!"

"As I told you, I didn't know you had relocated here until I read the newspaper article yesterday and I saw her obituary!"

Tad had heard enough. He placed his cane next to the doorway and forced himself upright, making himself tall and intimidating as he entered the headmistress's office.

"Excuse me, Miss Medlock," he said in a booming voice as he entered the doorway unannounced.

"I'm busy, Tad. What is it?" Medlock snapped.

"Just wanted to inform you that Miss Clarkson was not the cause of the fire yesterday. I examined the phonograph, and it was the old power cord that had shorted out. She was not to blame."

"Thank you, Tad. That will be all," Medlock replied with a dismissive tone and flick of her wrist.

Tad stood unmoving in the doorway.

"Anything else?"

"Yes. You paddled Katie unjustly yesterday for something she didn't do. She deserves an apology."

"That will be *all*, Mr Turly!" Medlock said, slamming her hands down on her desk.

Tad, without even a flinch of emotion, turned to leave, looking deeply into Theresa's eyes with a slow nod, as though he were trying to tell her something important.

Theresa got the message. She also had noticed the wooden paddle with holes drilled in it hanging on the wall behind the headmistress's desk. A thought came to her. *So there is a Katie and a Turly.*

Theresa stood looking into the cold, hollow eyes of Medlock. Images flashed in her mind of confrontations between Mina and the woman. *Were those actual memories?*

"Good day, Miss Medlock," she said, walking out without waiting for a reply.

Theresa frantically looked about for the man who seemed to be trying to tell her something. Tad was nowhere to be seen. After a deep sigh and feeling quite defeated, Theresa headed for her car. As it came into view, she noticed something tucked beneath the wiper blade. She looked about to see if its author was nearby, and then something caught her eye. A girl and a boy. They were in their early teens, and a shiver went up her spine at the sight of them. She somehow knew their names, Betty and Arthur.

Suddenly Theresa seemed to be moving in slow motion as a fresh memory flashed upon her mind.

The two teens had coaxed Mina down to the cellar of Saint Austin's under pretence of friendship. They had always mocked and mistreated Mina, but now they were pretending to be her friends, promising her chocolate. They led her to an unused storage room and dared her to go inside to find a big surprise.

Arthur slammed the old wooden door behind her, leaving her in total darkness with a dozen mice squealing at her feet. Betty then wedged a bit of wood under the door, trapping her inside.

Mina cried and banged on the door whilst Betty and Arthur laughed about it to each other, leaving Mina to her despair.

That very night the bomb struck Saint Austin's Orphanage. The first strike on the orphanage shifted the doorframe enough for Mina to escape the room. The second buried her in the rubble.

Theresa felt sickened by this memory, but was it real? She turned back, intending to confirm their names, but they had already vanished around the corner of the main building.

She pulled the note from the wiper blade. It read:

> *If you want information about Mina,*
> *meet me at the Cork at 1800*
>
> *Turly*

"Damn," she mumbled to herself. "Why did it have to be the Cork?"

The Cork was an ancient pub. Its thick wooden frame and crossbeams gave it a warm and welcoming appeal. The slatted wood floors gave off a distinctive smell of old beer and pine. The windows of the pub were dirty and contained warped and pitted glass from another era, which distorted everything on the other side.

It was several minutes after six p.m. and quite dark outside as Theresa entered the tavern, drawing the cold air in with her. She wore her scarf on her head, obscuring most of her facial features. Her black peacoat looked well-worn and was missing several buttons. Theresa shivered, rubbing her hands together as she closed the door behind herself.

She prayed no one she knew would notice her. She looked about for

Turly and, seeing that he had not yet arrived, quietly seated herself at the far booth with her back to the crowd.

The barmaid approached her to offer service. She was a heavyset, middle-aged woman with heavy breasts that hung low. Theresa knew it was Millie by the sound of her footfalls.

"Whah'll it be fer yeh?" Millie asked.

Theresa, keeping her head down, simply replied, "A pint of stout."

The woman quickly crouched down to eye level with Theresa and spoke in a whispered tone. "Whuh ah yeh doin 'ere, Tree?" she said with great fear in her voice.

"Meeting someone!" Theresa whispered back.

"You've goh'a geh out of 'ere! Jimmy and the boys always come in after work. If he sees yeh, 'e'll tell Tom! You've goh'a go out the back way… now!"

"I wouldn't be here unless it was important, Millie!" Theresa said. "I'm trying to find a runaway child. I'm meeting a man named Turly who has information that might help me find her."

Millie stood back up, her eyes darting nervously around the room. Turning back to Theresa, she took a deep breath and whispered, "You be careful, Tree. I'll geh your pint."

Theresa lit a cigarette with trembling hands. She could hear Millie drawing her pint from the keg on the wall. She heard the door open and after a moment heard Millie call out.

"'Allo, Mr Turly! Thu usual fer yeh?" Theresa heard a quiver in her voice.

Theresa turned her eyes to the door where Tad was now standing. A look of concern covered his face as he greeted Millie. She wore a false smile and a look of fear in her eyes. Millie nodded toward Theresa's booth. Tad nodded and hobbled over to where Theresa sat, his cane making a *clunk* sound on the wood floor every other step taken. He seated himself across from Theresa, concern in his eyes as he realised she wasn't supposed to be there.

Hilary and Katie crouched in the darkness of the snicket adjacent to the Cork. Tad had told them sternly not to follow him to his meeting with the mystery woman. They ignored him, of course, and followed on foot.

It had begun raining again but for the moment without more snow. They both shivered in the damp cold.

"You fink Mina's really alive?" Katie whispered with bulging eyes as the girls peered through warped glass, watching Old Man Turly and the mystery woman.

"I'm hopeful," Hilary replied.

"'Opeful? What the 'ell does that mean? 'Opeful? Shut up!'"

"I wonder who she is," Hilary muttered to herself.

The girls had to keep moving their heads around to different places in the warped window glass as things inside looked so distorted. Tad was sitting at a wooden booth in the far corner near the doorway to the loo. The woman's back was to them, and they couldn't see her face behind the maroon scarf.

Tad had his long-stemmed pipe out, with a cloud of smoke surrounding him. He looked like a Dickens character to Hilary. Nearly a half hour had passed, and the girls were ready to burst with curiosity about the conversation between Old Turly and the stranger.

The girls' attention was suddenly interrupted by a group of loud men approaching. They smelled of fish. Hilary guessed they were fisherman wanting a pint or three before heading home. The leader was a thin, ginger-haired man.

The profane group entered the Cork, nearly shoving Katie onto Hilary's lap in their rush to enter through the pub's narrow wooden doorway at the same time.

"Oi! Tosser!" Katie cried out.

Hilary watched as they instantly began barking out orders to Millie, apparently expecting her to drop everything and rush over with their pints and a smile. After several minutes, the ginger-haired man grew quiet and began staring at the mystery woman whose back was turned to him.

After downing his pint in a single gulp, he quietly hurried out the door, nearly crushing Hilary and Katie again, and disappeared into the darkness.

Hilary and Katie looked at each other in silence. Something was very wrong.

"I'm sensing some history here with these blokes and you, Theresa," Tad said in a low voice.

Theresa nodded. She put out her cigarette. "Let's go out the back way."

Tad agreed, but it was too late. Tom now stood at her table with his bloodied butcher's apron still on. Jimmy, the ginger-haired man, stood behind him, chewing his fingernails beyond the quick.

"Well, well, what 'ave we got here?" Tom mused in that condescending, gravelly voice Theresa knew so well.

Theresa slowly looked up. Standing before her was the devil—black and red, ugly, evil, with horns and a tail. She blinked. Now she saw Thomas, older, fatter, the bags under his eyes even fuller and a deeper shade of purple than she remembered.

"Thomas," she said as a sickening nausea filled every cell in her body.

"Hello, luvah. Miss me?" he said with a wink. "So you fancy old coots now, eh, Theresa?"

She remained silent. Tom slowly picked up Tad's cane from the corner of the table. He studied the intricate bone hand grip for a moment with seeming admiration, looked at the old man with an evil smile and in a flash, struck him across the face. The old man crumpled into a pile on the floor, unconscious.

Tom then turned his eyes and cane to Theresa.

Chapter Thirty Two

The Meat Locker

THERESA OPENED HER eyes. For a time, she lay motionless, her eyes slowly opening and closing, feeling and thinking nothing.

Her first sense to awaken was her hearing. She heard the metallic whirring of a motor above her. Her eyes drifted about the darkness. After several minutes, she began to feel a deep throbbing pain in her damaged shoulder and on the side of her head. She realised she was lying on her side, atop the shoulder she had injured when the support beam of the porch had collapsed on her, an event which now seemed so long ago.

She rolled onto her back and felt her head with her fingertips, trying to locate the source of the pain. A huge knot stood at attention above her ear. Then she remembered; Thomas had struck her.

Theresa struggled to a sitting position, feeling like she was moving through water. Suddenly her remaining senses came alive. She began shivering. Her hands and face felt sticky and numb. She recognised the sound of the motor running above her. She was in Thomas's walk-in fridge. His meat locker, as he called it. He must have carried her back to his butcher's shop and dumped her inside. She knew huge chunks of fish and lamb hung from hooks near her, unseen by her eyes in the darkness. Theresa knew this place all too well. There was no working latch inside that would set her free. She was a prisoner. A sense of panic filled her heart.

After several deep breaths to calm herself, she decided to stay quiet until she had fully regained her senses and could try to figure her way out. She knew if she started pounding on the door, Thomas would come. She wasn't prepared for that confrontation… yet.

"I'm fine! I'm fine. No need to make a fuss, I'm fine!" Tad protested as Katie and Millie helped him to his feet and out of the pub. Katie spotted Hilary running toward them as Tad again protested, "Let me be! I'm fine!"

"Well?" Katie demanded from the winded Hilary.

"The man took her to a butcher shop!" Hilary cried out.

"You have to get 'er out of there. He *will* kill her!" Millie's tone reflected genuine fear.

"We need to phone the rozzers!" Katie said.

"No!" Millie said. "We 'aven't any! This is a small fishing village. All the police we had are now fighting the Germans. Tom and Jimmy run it. You 'ave got to get 'er out!"

"Which way is the butcher shop?" Tad demanded, rubbing his sore jaw.

"Next street over," Hilary said, still panting heavily. "Shortcut through the snicket, left into the alleyway, and his back door is second on the left. Door is painted black."

"Let's go." Tad hobbled forward as quickly as he could without his cane.

"Whoa, Mr Turly! You're in no condition for this!" Hilary exclaimed. "Let me and Katie take care of it!"

"You two? Don't be daft!" he retorted. "I'm stouter than I look!"

The heavy rain had begun as they approached the back door to the shop. Tad halted, his white hair matted to his swollen face. With great focus, he studied every detail of his surroundings—the buildings, metal stairways, clusters of dustbins, dimensions of the snicket and larger alleyway, and even the stones and gravel at his feet. After a long moment, with the girls growing ever more impatient, he revealed his plan.

"All right, listen up. We need a distraction, something to draw him away long enough to get Theresa out of there."

Tad looked at Katie. "Can you run fast?" he asked pointedly, staring deep into her eyes.

Katie smiled a toothy grin. "Faster than a horse with mustard stuck up iz bottom!"

"Good," he said as he stooped down to gather several stones. With a wince, he stood back up, examining the stones carefully. "Here's what you're going to do…"

Tom's face was still beet red as he carved up several pork roasts and wrapped them in paper. As he moved around his wooden cutting table, his feet made squishy sounds on the filthy floor, which was covered in animal blood, discarded fish heads, pigs' feet, and rat droppings. He mumbled to himself angrily, his face occasionally twitching into a sneer. Glenn Miller played on the old radio in the corner of the front counter.

Suddenly the lights went out and then the radio and finally the rattling motor to the walk-in fridge. For a moment Tom stood silent, his bulging eyes darting about.

The light from a small streetlamp across the road shone through his front window. The cold light on Tom's face made his features look bluish and even more harsh.

Tom realised it wasn't a power outage for the entire town; it was just his building. He quickly headed toward the back door as the fuse box was outside. "Someone's tampered with it. Must be an enemy," he mumbled.

In the darkness, he fumbled for his shotgun but couldn't find it, so he opened the back door with his fists clenched as weapons instead.

The fuse box was to the right of the door, down about six feet, mounted on the building's brick wall. He peered inside the already open box. All the fuses were gone.

He spun about, scanning for anyone who might be the thief. He wiped the stinging rain that was dripping into his eyes. His focus quickly zeroed in on the four metal dustbins. He started moving slowly toward them, his knuckles cracking.

Suddenly a voice at the end of the alleyway rang out, "Iz this what you're looking foh, fat man?"

Tom turned to see a girl at the far end of the alleyway. She tossed two of the fuses at him. They landed with a plop in a rain puddle far short of him. She began laughing as she turned and ran.

Tom stampeded after her, his head down like a bull, stomping through the puddles. The girl disappeared round a dark bend. As Tom rounded the corner, he stopped with a jolt. Tad stood before him with great fury in his bruised and swollen face. As Tom charged, Tad, with lightning speed, threw a single black stone, hitting Tom squarely between the eyes. Tom crashed to the ground in a pile and lay still.

"You understand what to do if he wakes up?" Tad demanded.

"Aye," Katie replied.

"Across the street in the alley and in the shadows is where you stand. No closer! Understand?"

"Aye."

"Ten minutes. All I need is ten minutes. After that, or if he wakes up, you make a run for it. Got it?"

"Aye."

"Take this. It's my pocket watch. Look at the time. Ten minutes from now. No more! If he even twitches, you run like your arse is on fire to the butcher's shop. If he sees you, keep going. I'll deal with him. Understand?"

"Aye."

"Don't get caught."

"Aye. I won't."

"And don't let him see your face! I don't want him coming after you. Damn, I don't like involving you in this," Tad said, looking down on the now dribbling Thomas. Tad and Katie nodded at each other.

She watched Tad shuffle back down the dark alley toward the butcher shop. She looked at Tad's fob watch and shook her head. "He's not gonna make it."

Whilst Tad and Katie had drawn Tom away from his shop, Hilary snuck in the back door.

"Theresa?" she whispered. "Theresa! I'm a friend of Mr Turly. I'm here to help. Theresa?"

Tad hurried as quickly as his hip would allow. Desperately wishing he still had his cane, he used the brick wall for support as he neared the black door. After a deep breath, he entered the butcher shop.

"Hilary! Theresa!" he called out in a booming voice.

"She's not here, Mr Turly! I've searched everywhere!" Hilary said, her voice laced with fear.

Suddenly banging and muffled screams could be heard from inside a metal box. Tad and Hilary hurried over to the meat locker and began pulling on the handle. Finally it opened, and Theresa stumbled out, her face and hair covered in frost.

Katie looked at Turly's watch again under the streetlamp: twelve minutes. The big orangutan still lay in a puddle of his own drool. Time to go… past time to go. Tad's plan had worked to perfection. She felt quite pleased with her part in it as well. As she strolled across the street toward the rendezvous, she looked back to where Tom lay. A chill ran up her neck. He was gone.

"Hello, poppet," a voice whispered in her ear.

A sick feeling flooded her being as she suddenly felt an arm grasp her around the middle and lift her off the ground, turning her sideways.

Katie hung limply like a cat under Tom's arm as he closed and locked the back door of the shop. He plopped her down on the front counter. She sat frozen in fear as he rummaged through her coat, retrieving several of the remaining fuses and Tad's fob watch. He tossed the watch to the floor near the front window.

Tom reached under the counter and pulled out a small red box. He gathered two replacements for the ones Katie had tossed at him. He stared unblinkingly into her eyes.

Katie opened her mouth and words fell out. "I'd like a 'alf pound of bacon… to go please."

Tom slammed his hands down on the counter on either side of her in obvious fury. Katie began shaking.

"A little thief! Tha's what you are!" he screamed angrily. "You're one of those little brats from that orphanage, aren't you?" His eyes burned through her. "I can see why your parents dumped you! Worthless little shit!"

Suddenly Tom stopped, frozen in place. His eyes bloated and moved to the back room where the meat locker was. He turned and started toward it, then stopped again. Tom grasped Katie by the arm, yanking her down from the counter onto the floor, nearly pulling her arm out of the socket.

He wrapped his giant hand around the back of Katie's neck, his thumb and middle finger nearly touching as he led her toward the meat locker and pulled the latch open on the door. In the faint light, he could see it was now empty.

"Where is she?" Tom roared, shaking Katie violently. Katie stood silent, her eyes bulging out in fear at the demon before her.

Tom hurried her back to the counter and shoved her beneath it. The floor was sticky and smelled foul of animal blood. Katie scrunched into a little ball and began crying.

"What's your name?" Tom demanded.

"Kay... Kay'ee," she replied with a shaking voice.

"Who helped you steal my property, Katie? Was it that old man?" he said, hovering menacingly over her.

Katie was terrified. The cold light from the streetlamp shined on Tom's face. She saw Satan standing before her.

Tom looked up toward the window. Katie peered through a small knothole in the plywood counter to see what had temporarily redirected the man's anger. A shadowed figure was standing directly in front of the windowpane. The figure was that of a child, soaked to the bone, all dressed in black.

Her hair was long and lay flat against her head and face from the rain. She looked pale and ghostlike. She stood motionless and stared, unblinking, into Tom's eyes.

"Whuh the...?" he mumbled and slowly walked around the counter to the front window facing the ghost child. Thomas crooked his head, much like an animal sizing up its prey, and leaned forward toward the warped glass, his red eyes bulging.

"Lucy?" he mumbled quietly.

Katie peered over the counter for a better view, her hands still shaking. It was Mina! She and Tom were engaged in a staredown through the glass. They both stood motionless for a long moment.

Suddenly Mina let out a horrible, high-pitched, shrieking sound that Katie had never heard before. Mina's eyes and face looked terrifying as the sound shattered the glass inward, blasting Tom backward and onto the floor, showering him.

Katie scrunched back down under the counter and clapped her hands tightly over her ears.

It was now silent except for the sound of the rain. Katie remained in place for a moment, too afraid to move.

Shaking all over, she slowly crept out from under the counter and looked about. Mina was gone. Tom lay motionless on the floor with chunks of glass embedded in his face and body, blood oozing from every wound.

Katie tiptoed on the crunching glass past Tom. She picked up Tad's fob watch and looked down at the unconscious man.

"Fohget the bacon. This establishment is decidedly unsanitary."

Katie stepped through the opening where the window had been. She looked about for Mina before darting away.

Chapter Thirty Three

Turly's House

THE EARLY DAWN light shone through the dirty round window of the old livery stable, which was now being used as the maintenance building at Elbry House as well as Turly's private residence. It still smelled of wood and old hay. Whilst it had been months since Saint Austin's had been destroyed and most of the staff relocated to Elbry, Tad had little time to set up a proper place for himself to live. He had sectioned off a small corner with old blankets and several tarpaulins as walls. A small cot served as a bed. An old wood-burning stove stood in the centre of the room to dispel the chill from the cold Scottish nights. He referred to it as his house. It wasn't really a proper home, but calling it that gave him a sense of belonging.

Theresa awoke after only a few hours' sleep. Hilary had remained by her side throughout the night, caring for her. She dipped the flannel into the water bowl and rung it out again before gently placing it back on Theresa's forehead. The water was slightly pink from blood. Theresa's right eye was nearly swollen shut. A dark purple circle surrounded it.

"I'm Hilary," she said with a smile.

"Theresa. Thank you so much for your help, Hilary. You didn't have to do this. Where are we?" She sat up on the squeaky cot.

Tad peered over Hilary's shoulder. "You're safe, Theresa. You're amongst friends." His own face was swollen and purple from his encounter with Tom as well.

"I'm so sorry to have involved you in this," Theresa said, dropping her gaze to the ground. "Thomas and I have a bit of history."

"I gathered that. Not the friendliest bloke, is he? No worries. Try to relax," Tad said. "Hilary just made a quick run over to the main building for you." He reached up upon a wooden countertop and retrieved a food tray.

"I suspect it's a bit cold now, but it's filling and just what the doctor ordered."

"Medlock is looking for you, Mr Turly," Hilary said.

Tad nodded, grasping his spare cane. "I'll get this over with. Back in a mo," he said, using the cane to part the blanket wall.

"Katie should have been here by now," Hilary said. Tad nodded with deep concern in his face as he shuffled out of sight.

34 Chapter Thirty four

The Scar

THERESA LIFTED THE top of the metal tray. She seemed quite pleased with what she beheld—two eggs, several slabs of bacon, toast with a pat of butter, and hot tea. She smiled at the sight and quickly engulfed the meal.

"That was wonderful! Thank you," Theresa said.

"You're most welcome," Hilary replied. "So um, may I ask you a question?"

Theresa nodded.

"Um," Hilary asked meekly, "did he do that to you? That... man?" She pointed to the long scar that ran from Theresa's cheekbone to the corner of her mouth.

Theresa nodded, smiling a smile of deep pain. "He's my former husband."

Hilary put her head down, nodding at the floor. "I heard... We all have heard about that man and his brother."

Theresa stared into space as her mind flashed back to that horrible evening many years ago.

It was late autumn. Most of the leaves had changed to yellow and red. Many now lined the forest floor. Theresa was running as fast as she could through the leaves, faster than she had ever run before. The branches and twigs gave way under her, crunching beneath her feet as the evening light receded into the darkness.

She held her left hand to her face, blood gushing between her fingers and down her forearm, leaving a trail almost anyone could follow. Dusk had been replaced with total darkness when she arrived at Melody's house.

Theresa pounded on the front door, leaving blood prints on the aged wood. Melody opened the door as Theresa stumbled in. She covered her mouth, letting out a scream of horror that frightened even Theresa.

"Oh my God, Tree. What did he do to you this time? Oh my God!" Melody's voice shook as she led Theresa to the kitchen.

She quickly pulled out a chair and sat her down. Theresa felt woozy as the room began to spin.

"Stay with me! Focus!" Melody commanded, her voice sounding muffled in Theresa's ears.

Theresa didn't recall falling onto the floor. She awakened several times to see Melody working above her, her friend's hands and forehead now covered in her own blood.

Theresa remembered feeling little tugs on her face as Melody sewed the two flaps of her cheek back together. She recalled choking on the blood that drained down her throat and vomiting it back up into a bowl some hours later.

The image of Thomas dragging her from their house by her hair onto the gravel road, the feel of his pocketknife being thrust into her mouth and slicing her cheek in two, played repeatedly in her mind. Thomas left her lying on her back in the street, directly in front of their house. Neighbours watched in horror as the man left her to drown in her own blood.

Theresa sat motionless, holding her cup of tea, staring ahead as the nightmare replayed in her mind. She felt sick inside revisiting it, something she had tried to forget for many years but was reminded of every time she looked into the mirror. No amount of makeup could cover the scar, neither outwardly nor inwardly.

Hilary stood silently watching Theresa stare off into space, deep in thought. "Are you all right?" she asked, placing her hand on Theresa's shoulder.

Theresa snapped back to the moment, blinking several times. "Yes, yes, I'm fine. Sorry."

Silence filled Turly's house, a silence which seemed very loud and awkward to Hilary.

After what seemed like an eternity, they heard a sound from the other room, the sound of footfalls racing toward them. Fear arose in their hearts; was it *him*?

The blanket wall was jerked aside. It was Katie, looking ghostly pale but whole.

Chapter Thirty Five

Medlock and Turly

THE STAIRCASE BEFORE Tad seemed to go on forever. His body ached from head to toe, not only from the scuffle the night before but from the fact he hadn't slept at all. After he received an earful from Medlock, Tad planned on getting a bit of shut-eye. His duties would have to wait, but what about Katie? A rescue must be mounted immediately.

Using his wobbly cane as support, he ascended the stairway toward Medlock's office. Two steps, rest a moment. Two steps, rest a moment. Finally, after what seemed like miles, he reached the top. Tad felt very old and frail. He was hunched over more than usual and relying heavily upon his cane.

The upper hallways were busy with children scurrying about, whilst the main level was quiet, with the residents still having breakfast in the dining hall. At this moment, he felt more like one of the frail residents downstairs than the maintenance man. The children stared at him with an occasional gasp as they crossed paths with him—he saw in their expressions that he did not look well.

The small shingle that read HEADMISTRESS above Medlock's door seemed to take an eternity for Tad to reach. He stopped just shy of the doorway.

As usual, Tad propped his cane just outside the door and stood up as straight as he possibly could. He now stood well over six feet tall as he entered Medlock's office.

Medlock sat silent for a moment, obviously taken aback at his appearance.

"Please sit down, Mr Turly," Medlock commanded.

"Thanks, I'll stand," he replied, knowing that if he sat down, he would have to struggle to get back on his feet. He didn't want to show Medlock any sign of weakness or frailty.

"I understand you instigated a brawl in a pub last night over that Collins woman, Mr Turly. Aren't you a bit old to be picking fistfights with men half your age?" she said, folding her arms before her.

"I did not," Turly replied curtly.

"That woman is trouble, Turly. Why were you talking to her?" Medlock demanded.

"We ran into each other at the boozer, had a chat and a beer. It's her ex-husband that's trouble, not her, *and* for what it's worth, ma'am, my private life is none of your concern," he replied, his face like stone.

Medlock's lips became more pursed as she stood. She folded her arms again as she walked up to Tad, who towered over her.

"Your job is in jeopardy, Turly. Do you understand that?"

He folded his own arms, looking down upon Medlock. "You want to sack me? Go ahead! You can take out the rubbish, you can fix the machines, you can haul the soiled linens to the laundry, and you can keep the vehicles tuned and running!"

Medlock stood silent for a moment.

"I've heard about that local man, the butcher and his brother," Medlock said, her tone much more sedate now. "I suggest you avoid him in the future, Mr Turly. That will be all." Medlock turned her back on him and seated herself at her desk.

"Ma'am," he said with contempt as he turned to go.

"One last thing, Turly," Medlock said. "Is the Collins woman all right?"

"He nearly killed her," he replied without looking back.

Katie's Coffee

THERESA AND THE girls busied themselves whilst Tad was gone.

As Katie shared her story, Theresa tidied up, though what she really needed more than anything was sleep.

Katie, in her very animated way, talked about how Mina had suddenly appeared from nowhere, used her *magical powers*, and shattered the glass, knocking Tom unconscious so she could escape, how she'd hid for hours on a nearby rooftop whilst Tom and Jimmy charged up and down the alleyways and streets, searching for her.

Theresa, with Mina's whereabouts and safety weighing on her, silently changed the bed linens that had been soiled with her blood. She also borrowed one of Tad's oversized flannel shirts to replace her own soiled blouse—she hoped he wouldn't mind. Theresa sent Hilary off to find him to let him know Katie had returned safely and that Mina was somewhere nearby.

Tad's makeshift bathroom wasn't terribly private, but she was pleased to find it functional and clean. With a fresh flannel cloth, she gently washed the dried blood from her face after pulling her hair back with a piece of ribbon Hilary had offered her earlier.

She stared hard into the mirror at her swollen features. *Wretched. Absolutely wretched. How has my life come to this?* she thought as a tear slid down her bruised cheek.

Despite Katie's traumatic experience, she seemed quite herself again, though a bit jumpy. Whilst Theresa had been freshening up in the loo, Katie wandered out into the shop area. On a wood bench that Old Turly used as a kitchen counter, Katie spied what she had been searching for: the coffee percolator! She smiled a big, toothy grin with a glint in her eye as she hoisted herself onto the counter. Katie pulled the top off the percolator and removed the inner container, promptly spilling old coffee grounds all over the counter. She dumped the remaining used grounds into a pile next to the percolator and began grinding up handfuls of coffee beans. After filling it with water and replacing the innards, the familiar *hiss-plop* sound began, and the smell of fresh coffee filled the room.

As Theresa pulled aside the curtain of the bathroom, Katie stood before her with a smile and a big mug of coffee.

"Why, thank you, Katie!" she exclaimed. "That was very thoughtful of you." Katie's eyes nearly disappeared behind her smile as she handed the mug to her. Theresa looked down at the thick brew. It reminded her of dirty motorcar oil. She reached for the spoon and began stirring it. *Thick as molasses,* she thought to herself while still maintaining her smile for Katie.

"Sorry, Theresa," Katie said apologetically, "but we 'aven't any cream or shugah!"

"Not a problem," Theresa said with a smile. "This is just the way I like it. Thank you."

Theresa stood for a moment, watching Katie, whose eyes were fixed on her in anticipation of Theresa's first sip. Theresa put the cup to her lips and pretended to take a big gulp. "This is perfect," Theresa said, hoping Katie would believe her. "It's just perfect!"

Katie pulled her mug of coffee down from the counter and began drinking it with delight.

Theresa's eyes toured the large maintenance building. Tools and motor parts were everywhere. Wash basins, broken toilets and piles of plumbing parts stood scattered throughout the room, waiting to be repaired or discarded.

Theresa stopped. Her eyes caught something just inside the big sliding door at the far end of the building. It was her car! She hurried over to it, with Katie following behind. Tad had replaced the headlamp, straightened the bent rim, and had been working on the engine. The bonnet was open, and Theresa could see that the timing belt had been replaced.

"He must have brought it over here during the night. What a kind man."

"Old Man Turly is the best!" Katie replied.

"That's 'Mr Turly,' Katie," Theresa said.

"Mr Turly is the best," Katie said, now visibly vibrating.

"Katie, how much of that coffee did you drink?"

Katie shrugged. "Ole of it!" she replied with a crooked smile.

37 Chapter Thirty Seven

The Predators and the Prey

TAD SHUFFLED TOWARD the main doors. Suddenly he stopped, turned, and followed his large beak-like nose into the dining hall. "Bacon and eggs!" he said to himself as he shuffled in. Tad never missed bacon and eggs for breakfast. This would be no exception.

After hanging his cane on his forearm, he gathered his tray, which had six extra slabs of bacon, a heaping pile of scrambled eggs, and a cup of tea, and sat down at an empty table. Tad carefully placed his eggs upon his toasted muffin, dashed them heavily from the nearby salt and pepper pots, and took a bite. He followed it with a slab of bacon, a few sips of tea, and began the process all over again. He felt better already.

Hilary crept across the grounds, hoping not to be spotted by Medlock or one of her humourless minions lest she experience the paddle. It was strictly forbidden for the children to go off campus, especially to the maintenance building.

As she approached the main entrance, she heard a commotion. There was some type of confrontation going on off to the side of the building near the playground.

Two men were interrogating the children, asking if they knew where Katie, Theresa, and a pale girl dressed in black were.

Hilary recognised Tom immediately. The fat man's face and arms were covered in cuts from the implosion of the glass last night, just as Katie had described him. One of his eyes had a blood streak extending from his pupil as well. The skinny man stood silent, chewing his fingernails bloody, looking quite anxious.

She listened intently for several minutes as the men demanded information from the kids, then quietly crept back toward the main door. Hilary hurried in, rushed up the staircase and down the long hallway toward Medlock's office; Medlock was alone at her desk. She checked in the janitors' closets and laundry room. She then hurried back down the stairs toward the dining hall.

Tad had just finished his meal when Hilary dashed in, looking about frantically. She spotted him and hurried over, her words spilling out all at once.

"I've been looking all over for you, Mr Turly! Katie's back! She's okay. She saw Mina too, but she's gone now."

"Who's gone, Katie or Mina?"

"Mina."

Tad sat for a moment. "That's wonderful news, Miss Hilary," he said, gulping down the last of his tea.

"There's more!" Hilary's excitement turned to fear. "Those two men are here. Here! They are asking about Katie and Theresa... Mina too!"

Tad sat deep in thought for a moment. Suddenly he stood. "Come with me!"

Chapter Thirty Eight

An Unexpected Ally

THERESA RECLINED IN an old wooden chair, rocking gently whilst enjoying her pipe. Katie, sitting on a nearby workbench, had stopped vibrating from the effects of nearly two litres of extra-strong coffee. Her eyes were getting very heavy, but she continued her chat with Theresa, which had now been going on for well over an hour. Tad was still gone. Theresa quietly worried if Medlock had given Tad the sack. This greatly troubled her. It would be her fault.

Theresa felt grateful that her tobacco pouch and old pipe had remained safe in her car. She tapped out the used remnants into a small dustbin nearby.

"I've nevah seen a lady smoke a pipe befoh," Katie said, eyeing the artwork on the pipe.

Theresa smiled. "It belonged to my father. At least I think it did," she said. "Do you want to see it?"

Katie nodded excitedly as Theresa handed it over to her. Katie studied the artwork intently. "You fink it did? Not shoh?"

"I don't remember my parents except for a vague memory of my father giving it to me and saying, 'Don't lose it. You'll need it one day,'"

Theresa said with a shrug. "I'm an orphan, like you lot. I grew up in Saint Austin's too, many years ago."

"Was Medlock headmistress then? She has to be like a hundred and eleventy-seventeen years old," Katie said with a chuckle and a snort.

Theresa smiled and shook her head. "No, it was a headmaster named Mr Murphy, an Irish bloke who had a chip on his shoulder. He had a little-man complex. He looked like a constipated leprechaun!"

"Ooh, me piles!" Katie joked, grasping her bum cheeks as she shared her interpretation of Mr Murphy.

They both laughed.

"Whuh 'appened to your parents, T'reeza?" Katie inquired, still engrossed in the pipe lettering.

"I don't remember. I've sort of erased it from my mental chalkboard." Theresa's voice had a deep sadness in it.

Katie looked up at Theresa. "I remember me parents. They were killed in a motorcar accident a couple of years ago. Miss me mum."

"I'm so sorry, Katie."

"Aye, me too."

There was a silence for a time as they were lost in their own thoughts. Theresa quietly rocked in her chair whilst Katie studied the pipe.

"This is the same lettering tha's on Mina's necklace," Katie eventually said.

Theresa nodded, remembering the night she had discovered it as well.

Katie handed it back to her. Theresa studied it for a moment before repacking it and lighting the fresh tobacco. She took a deep puff.

"Whuh does it mean?" Katie asked.

Theresa shook her head. "I don't know."

"How do you fink Mina got here befoh you? You 'ave a car?" Katie asked.

"I don't know. Perhaps she knew a shortcut off the roadway," Theresa replied.

"D'you fink she found me from one of her dreams?"

Theresa pulled the pipe from her mouth, resting it on her thigh, a slight chill running up her neck. She stared at Katie. "What do you know about Mina's dreams?"

"You've seen them come true, 'aven't you... ole of them?" Katie said.

"Did she do her fingers to the 'ead trick on you?" Katie imitated Mina, by holding two fingers to her own head and then motioning them toward Theresa's forehead.

Theresa nodded slowly.

Silence filled the conversation again. After a long moment, Theresa spoke. "I wish I knew what was going on with that child. I wish I knew where she was going."

Katie looked up at Theresa. "I know where she's going. She shared it wif me." Katie motioned with her two fingers again, showing the method by which Mina imparted the information.

Theresa's eyes grew wide as she sat forward in the rocking chair, facing Katie. "Where? Where is Mina going?"

Just then, the large wooden door slid open. Theresa and Katie looked toward the doorway, expecting Tad. It was Medlock.

"Oh, shit on a stick," Katie mumbled as Medlock entered the building.

"Language," Theresa rebuked in a hushed tone. She stood as Medlock approached. Tad entered the building behind her, obviously slowed by his hip.

"Mrs Collins," she said in her usual businesslike tone.

"Just Theresa, if you don't mind," Theresa responded politely.

Medlock looked at Theresa for a moment, noting her swollen face.

"I believe I understand why," she replied, an uncomfortable silence filling the room. "I'll get to the point, Theresa. Those Collins boys were just wandering about the campus, asking lots of questions about you and the girls. They've since left, but I have no doubt that they will be back, perhaps even tonight. You have not only endangered your life by coming here but the lives of my staff, children, and residents."

Theresa looked down at the ground. "I am truly sorry, Miss Medlock. That was not my intention in coming here. I honestly was trying to help Mina. I feel responsible for her," she replied apologetically.

Medlock seemed different now, almost human. "Well, what is done is done. My concern is for the safety of the children. Katie and Hilary are no longer safe here, and neither are you nor Tad."

They all turned suddenly toward the doorway at the sound of someone entering. But it was only Hilary, struggling in with several heavy boxes.

"Thank you, Miss May," Medlock said. "You can set them down."

Medlock continued, "You need to leave—all of you—by early morning at the latest. Mr Turly will accompany you and the children to a place of safety. I need you both to take Katie and Hilary to Cannich. I was on the telephone just now and have arranged for the girls to stay there."

Katie tugged on Theresa's shirt to get her attention. "We have to go there, T'reeza. We *really* have to go there."

"Why, Katie?" Theresa asked.

"'Cause tha's where Mina's going!" she replied.

"To Cannich?" Theresa asked.

"Nooo! The Caledonian Forest, but she has to go through Cannich to get there. We might be able to find Mina on the way."

Medlock folded her arms and turned her focus on Katie. Hilary now stood next to Theresa. "And just how do you know that, Miss Clarkson?"

Katie, looking back at Theresa, motioned her two fingers to her forehead. Theresa understood. Medlock shared a raised eyebrow of confusion.

"She's right," Hilary chimed in. "She shared it with me as well. That's where they found her, standing like a statue before she came to Saint Austin's."

"Standing like a statue?" Theresa said, unsure if she had missed part of the conversation.

Before Hilary could answer, Medlock inserted herself. "She was found in a catatonic, almost petrified state. At first they thought she was dead as they couldn't find a pulse on the child. Imagine their surprise when she sat up in the morgue with a tag on her toe two days later."

"What happened to her?" Theresa asked.

"Don't know," Medlock replied, almost dismissively.

Theresa thought for a moment. "Right then. I'll do it."

Medlock turned, pointed to the overflowing boxes that Hilary had brought in, and offered up final instructions.

"Take these supplies with you. There are blankets and warm clothes for the children as well as their personal belongings. It's still quite cold there this time of year. I suggest all of you stay inside here today. Don't go out of this building and try to—"

"Mina is out there, Miss Medlock," Theresa said. "She may still be nearby. I need to find her!"

"I've sent three of my best people out to search for her. They all know her on sight. If she's out there, they will find her. You, on the other hand, are being hunted by a madman who nearly killed you last night. I won't have you endanger any other lives, including your own. Are we clear? Stay inside and try to get some rest. You'll need to leave before sunrise tomorrow." Medlock paused for a moment and then turned to Turly. "Make sure her car is running well and brimmed with petrol."

Tad nodded.

"Thank you, Miss Medlock," Theresa said.

"Thank you for your kindness," Katie and Hilary echoed in unison.

"One last favour, if I may ask?" Theresa inquired. "I really need to use your telephone to ring my friend. Tell her where we are going. She'll be concerned."

Medlock motioned with her head for Theresa to follow.

After a few moments of silence, Katie spoke to Tad. "We thought Medlock gave you the sack!"

Tad gave a smile. "She can't sack me. I'm her boyfriend!" Both Katie and Hilary gasped, unsure if he was jesting.

Theresa's phone conversation was brief. She rang Melody at work as they had no telephone of their own, leaving out the details of the night before but stressed the importance of taking the two children to Cannich.

"Oh, before I ring off," Melody said. "I thought you should know."

"What, Mel?"

"Um… the day you left, I noticed your orchids have turned black," Melody warned. "They are still black."

"All of them? Theresa asked with a shaken voice.

"Yeah," Melody said. "She also put her acorns in all the windowsills. Be careful, Tree." With that, the call ended.

Medlock had posted four of the staff as lookouts throughout the day to ensure their safety and see the girls to the main building for dinner.

Shepherd's pie was being served in the dining hall. Theresa, Katie, and Hilary dined with Medlock at a large corner table.

Tad finished loading and securing all they would need for the road trip tomorrow. He still had not slept since his confrontation with Tom Collins the night prior. The reddish bags under his eyes seemed twice their normal size. He hoped he could sleep some tonight. After securing the last rope to the frame of Theresa's car, he looked over the map on the table one last time. After a moment, his bushy eyebrows merged into one. He placed one finger on the reference for Cannich.

"That can't be right…"

After studying the map, he moved his finger to another spot on the map some miles away. He tapped it several times, nodding to himself.

Tad gathered his cane and headed over to the main building to join the others for dinner. Normally he would have set his cane at the door and stood up straight, as not to look old to Medlock, but not this evening. He was simply too tired.

Tad sank silently into the chair next to Theresa, who was talking with Medlock. One of the staff spotted him and quickly brought over a plate of shepherd's pie, setting it before him with a smile. Tad breathed in the smell of it. He smiled to himself. Miss Hatchet made the best shepherd's pie, better than any pub fare to be had.

"I believe your assessment of Mina is correct, Theresa." Medlock sounded almost agreeable. "She has been telling her tall tales since she arrived at Saint Austin's, though I am amazed by her ability to keep her stories straight. Most troubled children like her tend to change their fantasy stories quite often, perhaps seeking attention if the first version of their events are dismissed or ignored."

Theresa nodded. "I wasn't aware that Mina's story making began before her coming to stay with us. I assumed it was from the trauma of what she had been through in the bombing. Children often reject traumatic events and replace them with something more manageable, even wild fantasies, as a coping mechanism, a way to survive emotionally."

Medlock listened intently to Theresa's words. It had been a very long time since she had someone, especially a female someone, whom she could talk to about such things.

"I also find your theory of her being a feral gypsy child intriguing," Medlock said. "That possibility had not occurred to me, and her knowledge of classical writings and folklore would seem to offer up some validity to your hypothesis. Where did you go to university, Theresa?"

"Ogden Styres in Scotland… It's up north. I have a degree in maths with a minor in psychology."

"Really? I attended Crossrun Gables. It's up north as well. It's a shame this town is such a hostile place for you. We could use someone like you here at Elbry."

"Most kind. Thank you," Theresa replied with a smile.

Hilary's eyes glazed over at all the psychobabble the two women were feeding each other. She despised intellectuals. *Blah, blah blah,* she mouthed silently to Katie.

Katie, in her overly dramatic fashion, sat with her palm resting on her cheek with a bored look on her face. Hoping someone was watching, she pushed her face into her hand, smooshing the skin ever upward. Eventually her head and arm plopped onto the table with a *thud*, as if she had fallen unconscious. She even feigned a loud snore, protesting the psychoanalysis that was going on at the dinner table. After a few moments, Katie began banging her head repeatedly on the wooden table, muttering, "I'm hitting me 'ead. I'm hitting the part of me 'ead that's up north."

Medlock sat quietly for a moment. "He did that to you?" Her eyes moved to the three-inch-long scar on Theresa's cheek.

Theresa nodded. "He blamed me for the death of our daughter. He wanted to make sure no one ever found me attractive again."

"I'm so sorry," Medlock said, closing her eyes.

The table became silent.

"If… if you find her, what will you do?" Medlock asked after a time.

Theresa seemed stunned. She hadn't thought of that. What would she do?

"I... I personally would like to have her stay with us. She might be a bit of a mess, but I do care about her."

"You know," Medlock said, "in times of war like this, finding orphaned children loving homes can be very difficult if not impossible. Most of these kids, especially the older ones like Hilary and Katie, will grow up on work farms or in orphanages, having no one to love and guide them... They grow up alone. Adopting older children can be a wonderful gift, not only to the child but to you as well. Something to think about."

Theresa was speechless. Was Medlock suggesting that she and Mel could adopt Mina, perhaps Katie and Hilary too? Thoughts and questions rushed through Theresa's mind. Far too many for her to give an answer right now.

"I'll give it some thought, Miss Medlock. Thank you," Theresa said with her eyes tearing up again.

Medlock smiled and stood to take her leave. The conversation had hit both Katie and Hilary squarely between the eyes. Even the thought of being adopted had long ago been abandoned by both girls. Was it possible that Theresa and her friend might even consider adopting them... all three of them?

Hilary quickly dismissed the thought as it seemed too good to be true. She didn't want to get her hopes up only to have them crushed.

Katie, on the other hand, sat glassy-eyed with a silly grin on her face. A home, to have a proper home again... could it be possible?

Chapter Thirty Nine

The Stranger in the Darkness

THREE LITTLE COTS were set up in the maintenance building: one for Theresa, one for Hilary, and one for Katie. It was late evening, and Tad had already retired to sleep.

Theresa tucked the two girls in after they had bathed, donned their nightgowns, and brushed their teeth. Theresa packed a few of their clothes and personal belongings in her own suitcase, which looked ready to explode at any moment. Hilary had to sit on the bulging suitcase so Theresa could fasten the latches. She hoped it would hold until Cannich.

After a final cup of tea and a bowl of tobacco from her pipe, she lay down next to the two girls on her undersized cot and drifted off to sleep. Disconnected dreams filled her mind throughout the night as she tossed and turned.

The night was cloudless as the nearly full moon shone through the tall window, casting a bluish hue upon Theresa's face as she slept. As the hours passed, the moonlight moved off to illuminate one of the workbenches nearby.

Silently a lone figure crept into the room. The creaking of the wood floor announced each step as the figure moved toward Theresa, each step becoming louder as it approached. The figure, shrouded in darkness, now stood above Theresa, watching her sleep. After several moments, it raised its arm and moved toward her, grasping her shoulder. Theresa opened her eyes and gasped.

"Mina?" Theresa said in a loud whisper that woke Katie and Hilary. Both girls bolted up from their cots, Katie so fast that she fell off the bed and onto the floor with a *thud*.

"Arggg… I'm okay. Fanks for asking," she said after a moment.

Mina stepped into the moonlight, revealing her face as Theresa scrambled to her feet and grasped the child, squeezing her tightly.

"We have to go now!" Mina sternly warned. "They're coming, both of them. They know where you are, and they are coming!"

"Did… did you have a dream about this, Mina?" Theresa stammered.

"Yes," she said. "That's why I came back. They will be here soon, and none of you can be here when they come. We have to go now."

Theresa quickly dressed and commanded Hilary to wake Tad.

"Girls, get dressed and use the loo. We have to go!"

Tad stumbled out from behind the curtain, bleary-eyed and dishevelled. "What's going on in here?" he said, squinting at the newcomer.

"Mina?"

"Hi, Mr Turly," Mina replied. "We have to go."

Tad stood silent for a moment. "Good enough for me," he said. Tad moved the blanket aside and quickly dressed. By the time he returned, everyone was loading into the car. The old man had no time to ask Mina how she had found them or tell her just how delighted and relieved he was to see her.

Despite Theresa's doubts about Mina's so-called past, she had seen enough to know when to believe her. It was indeed time to leave.

Tad quickly unlocked the carriage doors and slid them open. Theresa backed her car out. Tad closed and relocked the doors and sat down on the passenger's side of the car with his cane. Mina, Katie, and Hilary sat cramped in the back seat.

They were off.

40 Chapter forty

Tom and Jimmy

IN THE EARLY dawn light, two figures crept up on the old maintenance building.

Tom Collins shouldered an axe and a large container of liquid in his oversized left paw. Jimmy shivered, looking about anxiously. Frost covered the red stable and the lock that protected its contents.

Tom looked about for any potential witnesses. His eyes burned with an angry fire. With the butt of the axe, he whacked the lock and latch. It popped off instantly. Jimmy slid the door open.

It was dark inside, with only faint rays of morning light penetrating the darkness. They hurried in, much like a military assault team, looking for anyone or anything that breathed. They searched every corner of the building but found no one.

"They've gone, Tom," Jimmy said.

"I can see that, idiot," Tom retorted.

Tom began pouring the container of petrol all over the floor and tabletops. "This'll teach them to help that woman. Bastards." Suddenly

Tom stopped. Something of great interest lay on the table before him, a map and an itinerary.

An evil grin spread across Tom's face. "Got you, bitch." He quickly folded up the map and travel plan and stuffed them into the back pocket of his sagging trousers.

He continued pouring petrol on everything with enthusiasm, recklessly splashing it on Jimmy.

"Oi!" Jimmy exclaimed, spitting petrol from his mouth and wiping it from his eyes.

"Well, stay out of my way, idiot!" Tom snapped. He poured a stream of petrol to ignite, leading to the doorway. He tossed the empty container inside.

"Let me do it!" Jimmy demanded. "Gimme those matches! I want to do it!"

Tom tossed the matches over to the little man, who stood near the wooden table. Jimmy opened the box and pulled a wooden match from it. He slowly struck it against the tabletop.

Suddenly Jimmy's clothes burst into flame and engulfed him in a ball of fire. Shrieking, he ran about the stable, trying to escape the fire that was so quickly consuming him, igniting everything in his path. Jimmy's hair and skin melted in flame before Tom's eyes.

"Jimmy!" Tom screamed in horror. Tom stood twitching all over, not knowing what to do. The fires quickly engulfed the building. Tom could no longer see Jimmy through the fire or hear his screams for help.

Jimmy was dead. His brother was dead, and it was Theresa's fault.

Tom turned and ran.

41 Chapter Forty One

Confrontation and Breakfast

THE OVERLOADED CROSLEY crawled along the roadway toward Cannich. Driving was slow going as the freezing rain had turned to snow, and a thick glaze of ice covered the windscreen, making it most difficult to see the road before them. They all sat quietly with their own thoughts for a time.

Tad, finding himself dozing, loaded his pipe and rolled a cigarette for Theresa. He lit it and handed it to her.

"Thank you, Tad." What Theresa really needed was a strong cup of coffee. She jokingly wished for some of the potent brew Katie had made the day prior. *That would wake me up!* she thought to herself with a slight smile.

Katie leaned forward, poking her head between Theresa and Old Turly's shoulders. "I could get out an' walk fasta than this!" she said.

"Be my guest!" Theresa laughed.

Katie sat back in her seat. After a moment, she turned to Mina. "You're late. Where the hell 'ave you been?" she demanded of her with folded arms.

Mina stared at her for a moment. In her best mocking imitation of Katie, she replied, "Oot and aboot."

Katie grasped Hilary by the sleeve. "I don' fink she's lowcul!" she said with dramatically wide eyes in a low, monotone voice.

After the laughter subsided, Theresa decided it was time to confront Mina for running away.

"Mina," she said. "Mina, why did you leave? I've been so worried about you." Theresa's tone was sincere. Her eyes welled up as she looked in the mirror at the troubled girl.

"You didn't want me. You were going to throw me away. I heard you both. You were going to have the police take me away." The wound from Theresa's rejection cut deep. "I decided it was time to go home."

"Where is home, Mina?" Theresa asked, hoping for the truth this time.

Mina looked hurt. "I told you, *Balynfirth* is my home."

"Hear her out, Theresa," Tad interjected.

"Don't humour her, Tad!" Theresa said angrily. "Mina, we both know that there is no such place as Balynfirth. You're not a mermaid or an elf. You're just a girl."

"Woods elf," Mina mumbled angrily under her breath as Katie began laughing.

"You told her that you're mermaid an' elf? 'Ow stewpid are you?" Katie exclaimed.

"Stop it!" Hilary demanded. "I believe her!" With that, she grasped and squeezed Mina's hand.

"Medlock will paddle you for that, Hils! Girls aren't allowed to hold hands!" Katie teased.

"I'm just comforting her, you nit!" Hilary replied angrily.

"Girls!" Theresa shouted. "Enough! I'm talking to Mina!"

Katie folded her hands on her lap and pouted silently.

"Believe what you want," Mina said after a moment. "I told you the truth."

"Mina, I'm sorry you felt rejected. It wasn't that we didn't want you. It was… well, I guess we were just… afraid."

"Afraid of me?" Mina said with a look of incredulity on her face.

"Erm… yes, but more afraid of the responsibility of caring for you. I'm so sorry. Please forgive me. Give me a chance to make it up to you please."

"That's what you said last time."

Silence filled the little car. The three girls nodded off, their heads bobbing about as they encountered bumps in the roadway.

They were all quite pleased when Theresa pulled off the roadway to a small town. Here they could get petrol and a proper bite to eat.

Medlock had given Theresa fifty pounds for spending money with the condition that she or Tad ring her from each stop along the way. The small eatery seemed like a good place for a quick meal.

The girls each enjoyed an egg, sausage patty, and a warm muffin with marmalade, which made them smile with delight.

Theresa and Tad spent much of their time at the table, holding their coffee cups to their noses and smelling the aroma as though it had magical healing powers. After breakfast, whilst the girls and Theresa used the lavatory, Tad rang Medlock at Elbry.

When the girls returned, Tad told them the news: The maintenance building had been burned to the ground, and a body was found within. They suspected the Collins boys, but there was no proof. The body was a mystery as well as it was charred beyond recognition. They quietly piled into the car and continued toward Cannich.

The next few hours were filled with a loud silence as everyone seemed lost in their own thoughts except for Mina. She slept soundly as the others thought about the news Tad had shared.

Tad looked exhausted and frail. Too much exertion and far too little sleep. Theresa felt great concern for him. Perhaps it would have been better if he had stayed at Elbry, but if he had, there might now be two bodies in the burned building instead of just one.

Deep inside, Theresa felt that this was all her fault, for by coming back in search of Mina, she had set this entire chain of events into motion. She again began to fear Mina. Trouble and death seemed to follow the girl everywhere. A chill ran up her neck as she revisited their conversation about Mina being a death dreamer.

Tad interrupted Theresa's thoughts by handing her another lit cigarette.

"Thank you, Tad," Theresa said with a weary smile. After a deep puff, she turned back to him. "Are you doing okay?"

"Fine, fine," he said. "I, for one, am looking forward to sleeping in a proper bed tonight!"

Theresa nodded with a smile. "No cot for you tonight, eh, Tad?"

He nodded, "Damn right!" He quickly covered his mouth with his hand. "Forgive my language, girls."

Chapter Forty-Two

A Good Night's Sleep

TAD RAPPED ON the frosted door with his cane. In the distance, he could see Arbroath Harbour through the frozen mist. The bitter cold cut through the others as they waited in silence for someone to open the door. Tad knocked again. A portly woman with round red cheeks answered with a warm smile. She was quite large for a woman, almost imposing to stand before. She had short, curly red hair and wore what seemed like an enormous piece of cloth that had been draped over her and sewn together to resemble a dress.

"Come in, come in! I was becoming concerned—the roads and all! I have a warm soup with bread and cheese waiting for you in the dining room. Come in!" she exclaimed in her high falsetto voice.

The group entered the house quietly. They hung up their coats and scarves and at Miss Thatcher's request removed their shoes and placed them in a tidy row next to the door.

"Oh my!" Miss Thatcher exclaimed with a jolly smile, clapping her hands together. "There are *three* children! Miss Medlock only mentioned *two*! Well, no problem. I have plenty of beds for each of you! Welcome, girls, welcome!"

Mina suddenly let out a loud gasp. Everyone turned to see what had startled her.

Miss Thatcher laughed nervously. "Oh, that's Basil! He looks like a wolf, but he's actually a husky. He doesn't bite, I promise. He's quite friendly."

Mina stared at the panting creature, its tongue hanging out the side of its mouth. "What's a Basil-Husky?" she said with a curious fear in her voice.

"It's a dog, Mina!" Theresa said with a smile.

Mina nodded. It reminded her of something fierce and cruel from her world.

"What does Basil-Husky do?"

"Well, he mostly just eats whatever food he can nick from the table and makes wee-wee messes!" Miss Thatcher said. Everyone but Mina laughed at this.

The meal was a feast. The little troupe of five had never tasted such excellent soup.

Miss Thatcher beamed. "It's called minestrone, with a side of Italian bread and cheddar cheese!"

She would only sit for a few moments at a time, often popping back up to refill everyone's soup bowls. She was intent on gorging them.

Tad seemed quite taken with Miss Thatcher. Theresa smiled as she noticed the look in his eyes for the woman. He hadn't stopped smiling since their arrival, and his pale blue eyes had a twinkle in them that Theresa had not seen until now.

The food and conversation were delightful. They feasted for nearly an hour as the cold darkness of the night set in. Frost and ice quickly obscured any view from the windows as it covered each glass pane with a solid glaze for the night.

After they had eaten the entire cauldron of soup and enough bread and cheese for a week, Miss Thatcher put on the kettle and set out a pretty crystal bowl filled with boiled sweets that she had made that morning for the children.

"The tea is made from mint and camomile. It will help all of you sleep soundly tonight!" she proclaimed.

After tea, she showed them to their rooms. Hilary and Katie found the little twin beds in their room luxurious and comfortable, with loads of blankets under which to snuggle deep. The pillows were filled with goose down, and they fell fast asleep within moments.

Mina and Theresa had to share a room. After tucking Mina in the enormous bed, Theresa opted for a bowl of pipe weed before retiring for the night.

Tad's room was very masculine, with large paintings of ancient mariners' ships at sea hanging on the walls and wallpaper of game hunters out hunting with their dogs.

Tad was delighted at the softness of his bed as well. He had not felt so comfortable in many years. He thought about the day's events and Miss Thatcher. "What a woman!" he muttered to himself as he dozed off to sleep.

Theresa awoke early and quietly dressed as not to wake Mina, who was curled up in a ball on the edge of the bed. Lying next to her, wrapped in Mina's arms, was Basil, fast asleep. Theresa smiled. She gently placed another blanket on the girl. Mina looked so small and innocent lying there, hardly the troubled child Theresa knew.

Theresa quietly descended the staircase toward the kitchen. She could smell food cooking and laughter; someone else was awake as well. As she entered, she saw Tad sitting at the small kitchen table, wearing a big grin. He sat tall and seemed much younger.

Miss Thatcher had much the same look in her eye. They certainly seemed to be hitting it off.

"Good morning!" Theresa said cheerfully, announcing her presence. "Can I help with breakfast?"

"Oh! Why yes, dear! You certainly can," Miss Thatcher said nervously in her treble voice.

"Theresa! Would you like a cup of coffee that Betty made? It has butter in it! You must have a cup," Tad said excitedly.

"Why, yes, Tad. Thank you very much."

Theresa sipped on the coffee that Tad had handed her, and her eyes grew wide. "Oh, this is most excellent. It doesn't even need cream or sugar!"

With that, Mrs Thatcher seemed much more at ease and smiled brightly again. "You could help with the pancakes, Theresa," she said cheerfully.

Theresa smiled and put on an apron, taking over the griddle duties.

After the pancakes were stacked high on the nearby plate, Theresa turned to Tad. "Would you mind waking the girls?"

"Not at all." He quickly rose and headed to the stairway without his cane. Mina greeted him at the top of the stairs.

"Good morning, Mr Turly!" she said cheerfully.

"Good morning, Miss Mina. I was just coming to wake you. Breakfast is ready. Hope you're hungry."

"Famished!" she replied with a smile.

"Before you go downstairs, I need to ask you about something."

Mina nodded.

"When you came here, you were found near Cannich."

"I guess." She shrugged.

"But that's not where you started, is it? You had a very long walk?"

Mina nodded with a guilty look in her eyes.

"Thank you, sweetheart," Tad said with a smile. "That helps a lot. Pop on down for brekkie. I'll wake Katie and Hilary and be right down!"

After a delightful breakfast, a relaxing morning, and most excellent lunch with Miss Thatcher, the group set off for Cannich.

As they pulled away, Miss Thatcher stood on the front porch, waving with a big smile. Everyone in the car turned and waved, calling out "thank you" to her. Tad just smiled, looking into Betty's eyes, holding his hand up.

Chapter Forty Three

Nightmare Road

HILARY WAS MISERABLE. She sat sandwiched between Mina and Katie with scarcely room to breathe. Katie, on her right, sprawled out as much as she could in the tight back seat. Hilary glared at her with her most intense glare.

Katie's head hung back on her neck as though barely attached, her mouth hanging wide open.

"Daniel… I'm so sorry, Daniel," she muttered under her breath, several tears running down her cheek and into her ear.

The accompanying snoring coming from Katie was deafening and reverberated in the little car. Hilary seriously considered stuffing one of her socks into Katie's mouth, but the fear of having a cold foot dissuaded her.

Mina, on Hilary's left, was twitching every few seconds and was obviously having one of her bad dreams. Occasionally Mina's elbow would jab Hilary in the ribs.

Mina's face was covered in sweat as her eyes moved about behind her eyelids in a rapid, uncontrolled motion. She moaned softly.

Hilary looked to the passenger's seat up front. Oddly enough, Theresa appeared to be having a bad dream as well. Her head turned back and forth as she mumbled under her breath. It almost seemed like the three of them were sharing the same nightmare.

Tad wore a look of desperate concern.

"Mr Turly," Hilary asked quietly, "is everything all right?"

"Fine, child," he said unconvincingly. "Everything's fine."

The truth was that Tad was lost. The rolling hills had long ago given way to an ever-thickening forest and narrowing gravel road. He was certain that he had placed the map and itinerary in the motor car, but now he couldn't find either of them after rummaging throughout the front seats. He had put to memory the first leg of their journey, but now, when he needed the map most, it was nowhere to be found.

Sometime back, they had come to a crossroad, which Tad had paused at for a long moment, trying to remember whether they should turn right or left. He chose left and now feared he had chosen poorly.

The sky was growing white as the evening and snow approached. They had not seen another car or even a horse-drawn carriage for several hours now—except for one lone vehicle that had been behind them since they had left Miss Thatcher's house that early afternoon. It had stayed behind them the entire journey—about a half mile back, but it was always there.

Sometimes Tad thought that the other car had turned off on some side road, but as soon as a straight bit of road was behind him, he would see its headlamps again in the mirror.

Theresa's dream was the same one she had dreamt a thousand times before: *She's in a forest. Some kind of social gathering with food and dance as the evening descends. A large fire has been built in a clearing deep within the forest. Dozens of people, young and old, dance to the Celtic pipes and drums, as the very young Theresa sits on a log with her father.*

A tall man with a beak-like nose, wild dark hair, and a thick beard approaches and begins talking to her father as he smokes his pipe. The man has an almost identical pipe poking out of his leather vest pocket. An argument ensues, and the man and her father take her to a sailing vessel on the shoreline. Her father seems very concerned and anxious, not at all sure if he's doing the right thing.

"I should be the one to take and watch over her. Not you. I'm her father!"

"You can't," the tall man says. *"You have to look after your wife. You have a responsibility to her and our people, especially now. The door is closing. It has to be now!"*

"I have a responsibility to her too. She's my daughter!"

"I'm sorry. I am so sorry."

"Why her?" he says over and over. *"She's a child. What can she do?"* Her father's voice is filled with grief and doubt.

"You know why. You've known since before she was born."

"How can you be sure about this prophecy? What if it's wrong? What about my little girl?"

"I will look after her. I'll make sure she's safe and cared for. I swear!" the man says.

After a time, Theresa's father concedes to the tall man, and just before they set sail, her father gives her his pipe to remember him by and makes her promise not to lose it. "You will need this one day," he warns her.

As the ship pulls away from the harbour, Theresa tries to jump in the water, screaming for her daddy. The tall man constrains her as she hits and kicks him frantically, her eyes fixed on her father, who's growing ever smaller on the pier.

Hilary's patience had expired. She simply couldn't take any more of Katie's snoring. She pinched Katie's nostrils together. Katie gasped, rocked her head, and snorted.

"Oi!" she cried out angrily.

Theresa suddenly awoke.

"Settle down, girls!" Tad commanded. "We'll stop soon so you can stretch your legs."

Theresa looked about her surroundings blankly. Her dream, as always, had been very intense. It often took her several minutes to return to reality.

"Did you 'ave a good nap?" Tad asked her.

When she didn't answer, he continued, "Would you mind filling my pipe? It's been several hours, and I'm really craving a bowl right now."

"Sure," she said.

Tad had already tapped it out, so it would be a simple task of filling and packing it. She pulled her own pipe from her jumper pocket to fill as well and then noticed something very odd. The writing on the base of Tad's pipe was almost identical to hers, with just a few differing symbols at the bottom of the wooden bowl. They were essentially the same pipe, certainly made by the same craftsman.

She felt her breath catch in her throat. Of what coincidence could this be that Mina's door key and these two pipes could have the same obscure language carved into them, a language that Mina claimed was from another world?

How were the three connected? Her recurring dream flashed before her mind's eye. The tall, bearded man whom she had been dreaming of her entire life bore a striking resemblance to Tad.

Theresa stared at the man next to her for a long moment.

"Who are you?" she demanded.

Suddenly Mina let out a scream as she awoke in horror, so startling that Tad swerved the car in surprise.

"Mina, what's wrong?" Theresa exclaimed.

Mina's face was covered in sweat, and she looked very pale. "He's coming! He's here!" she cried out.

Instantly they felt the car lurch forward violently whilst they were thrown backward into their seats. The car that had been following them rear-ended them again with even more force.

Tad tried desperately to keep control of the old Crosley.

Theresa looked to the car behind them. Thomas was at the wheel. Fire seemed to shoot from his swollen red eyes. The devil had found them again.

The car backed off for a moment to get a run-up on them. It struck the left rear corner of the Crossley, folding the wheel rim into the tyre, which exploded, shredding into ribbons. The car swerved and slid off the side of the road, bounding down the embankment, bouncing wildly over the rocks, and plunging bonnet first into the rushing river below.

The car turned onto its side, floated to the middle of the river, and quickly sank into the icy water.

Theresa pounded on the door, trying to open it, her face mashed up against the window glass in terror as the car sank beneath the icy water.

Tom stood on the edge of the riverbank as the car and its passengers disappeared into the river. He smiled, cradling his shotgun in his arms.

He watched for a moment as air bubbles rose from the water, not noticing the heavy sleet now falling and covering his hair in white pellets.

However, the fire within him did not subside. It only left him with an empty feeling, almost like walking through the remains of a home that had been burned to the ground and was now cold.

He fully expected that once she was gone, he would feel better, but he didn't. His hate continued to rage, but there was no one left on which to focus it. Tom felt sick and suddenly old. His brother was dead, and he had exacted his revenge. *Now what?*

Tom slowly walked back up the rocky slope, shivering a bit, now noticing the sleet covering the ground. His footprints were the only ones that would trail back up that hillside.

He paused at his car, noticing liquid pouring out from beneath the front end. His anger returned and boiled within his blackened soul. "Goddammit!" he cried out and cursed Theresa for the damage she had caused. Even in death, she tormented him.

The collision from hitting Theresa's motorcar had not only crushed in his radiator but broken the front axle. The left tyre was straight, but the right was now turned inward at an odd angle. His car wasn't going anywhere, and neither was he. He was stranded many, many miles from home, and it was all Theresa's fault. He wished he could kill her again… and again. He wished he could kill *all of them* again.

Tom looked back at the watery grave in silence. Suddenly something caught his eye on the other side of the riverbank; something or someone was moving away from where the car had sunk.

Tom stared intently at the water. "No," he said out loud. "It can't be."

Theresa opened her eyes as the overturned car filled quickly with the frigid water. In horror, she discovered Tad unconscious and slumped on top of her. Blood ran down his forehead from the impact on the steering wheel. The surrounding water was varying shades of pink and red.

She struggled to push him off as her face was now submerged under the rising water. With great effort and pain from her bad shoulder, she wriggled out from under him.

Within seconds, they were submerged. Theresa worked the door handle, frantically pounding on the door, but it was welded in place by the pressure of the water. She eventually abandoned it and began clawing at the canvas top. Shoving her fingers through several holes, she tore away the rotting canvas.

Theresa looked to the girls in the back seat. Their eyes, filled with terror, were fixed upon her. She motioned upward to them.

She could feel her lungs instinctively trying to draw air in as she ushered the girls out first. Katie grabbed the blue-faced Hilary by the collar and headed for the surface.

Desperately, Theresa tried pushing Tad up through the small opening, but darkness was surrounding her, and she felt her body going limp. She was out of breath. She was out of time. Suddenly she felt someone grasp and pull her through the opening. Mina motioned Theresa upward. With her last ounce of will, she rose to the surface, gasping and coughing up water. After a long moment, the darkness retreated, and she felt her strength and vision return.

Theresa drew a deep breath and then plunged back underwater to help Mina wrestle Tad to safety, only to find them both gone. The car was empty. In a panic, she rose to the surface again, looking all about. Hilary and Katie had just reached the bank of the river. Theresa was relieved to see they had chosen the opposite side from where Thomas was.

After a moment, she spotted Tad. He seemed to be floating toward the shoreline. She realised that Mina must be beneath him. She was holding his head above the water as they approached the shore. Theresa swam toward them as quickly as she could despite the excruciating pain in her shoulder. Mina remained underwater during the entire journey to the shore, not coming up for air even once.

Theresa grasped Tad, freeing Mina. They reached the sleet-covered bank. Katie and Hilary helped Theresa and Mina pull Tad from the icy water. He wasn't moving or breathing.

"Is he… is he dead?" Katie sobbed.

Theresa could see Thomas running back down the embankment on the other side, shotgun in hand.

Hilary and Katie looked pale and bluish, their teeth chattering. Time was short, very short, for all of them. If not because of Tom's shotgun, then hypothermia. Icicles now clung to their hair, and their clothing was quickly freezing to their skin.

Theresa had to make a choice: run or try to help Tad.

"Girls," she commanded, "get behind me and crouch down!" They obeyed her, scrunching into little quivering balls. "No matter what happens, stay behind me until he is out of shells!"

Theresa rolled Tad onto his back and began breathing air into his lungs as Thomas approached on the opposite shoreline. She could hear his shotgun being cocked. Tad suddenly lurched and began coughing up water.

There was no time to feel joy or relief. Theresa quickly sat him up and held his head as he continued expelling the water from his lungs. He was very weak.

Thomas approached the edge of the water, the long barrel of his shotgun pointed directly at Theresa. He stepped into her car's muddied tyre tracks. The typical Scottish squidge grasped his shoes and held on tight.

Tom suddenly lost his balance and fell face-first into the cold, dank mud. His shotgun flew from his hands and landed in the water between the shore and a rock. He began screaming curses at the freezing survivors whilst flailing in the sticky goo.

After slipping and falling several more times, Tom finally found his feet, but his shoes were now forever submerged in the squidge, his face and body covered in mud and dead grass.

The scene reminded Theresa of Buster Keaton films, but she couldn't laugh. Tom had spotted his shotgun. He scrambled over to it and pulled it from the water. After digging the mud out from his eyes and blinking them clear, he took careful aim.

Theresa looked about her surroundings for a place to hide, but there was none. The upper bank was too far away. They would never make it over the ridge in time.

"Stay behind me, girls. Stay as flat to the ground as you can." Theresa closed her eyes.

Above the sound of the rushing river, Theresa heard a *click*. She opened her eyes; Tom was glaring at his weapon, shaking it angrily. He took aim at Theresa again. This time she stared into his eyes. *Click*.

Tom let out a blood-curdling scream and began flailing his arms and stomping wildly again in anger.

Theresa and the girls stood and faced Tom. The powder in the shells of his shotgun was wet and wouldn't fire. Tom was across the river and couldn't swim. They were safe.

Theresa walked to the edge of the river and stared at Thomas as he continued his tantrum. She felt a deep calm.

She looked down at the water's edge. Several things from her car had washed ashore. She reached down and picked up her and Tad's pipes. Next to them was the leather bag of tobacco. The pipe weed was soaked but would dry out. Her lighter was still in her pocket, so at least she would have that, though she would have happily traded all of it for some shelter, food, and dry clothing for the others.

Theresa slowly walked back to her four shivering friends. Mina and Katie held Tad up on either side, each supporting him with their hands. The five of them climbed up the embankment, out of sight of the screaming demon.

"Why?" they heard him say. "Why won't you people just die?"

Night would soon be upon them, and finding shelter was critical. Hilary suggested they search the rock formations in the distance; it was their last hope of finding shelter. If they failed, they would die.

Hilary, Mina, and Katie could no longer feel their feet or hands but still took turns holding up Tad the best they could whilst Theresa supported him with her arm on the other side. He could barely walk. They journeyed in silence, often stumbling.

In the howling wind and bitter cold, Mina held on to the back of Theresa's jacket with her head down so as not to get separated from the group.

Visibility was only a few feet at best. They did not know if they were still heading toward the rocks. They might have already missed their only chance of survival.

Night descended.

44 Chapter forty four

The Cave

THE CAVE OPENING was narrow but negotiable. It had several sharp turns that helped create a barrier to the bone-chilling winds and snow.

Theresa crept in, using the only senses available to her, hearing and smell. The only source of light was from the falling iridescent snow that covered the ground and drifted up the side of the cave's entrance. Even that small amount of light soon dimmed as she felt her way through the opening. Several sharp turns and a sudden deep descent led to the chamber within.

Time was critical. The others were waiting just outside the opening in blizzard conditions. Theresa had to make haste.

She listened intently for sound, any sound—movement, breathing, anything. All seemed quiet except for the angry wind outside and the deep piles of dried leaves she shuffled through. Without the decaying force of nature, they had remained undisturbed since being blown in by the autumn winds. She sniffed the air for any sign of wild animals. There was only the smell of the leaves. She knelt down and felt them; they were still intact. If an animal lived here, the leaves would have surely been crushed to powder by now.

Theresa pulled her lighter from her coat pocket. She hoped against all hope that it would light and reveal the secrets of the cave.

Flick, flick, flick! The flint was still wet; it would not light nor even spark. She tried several more times with the same result. She felt her way back out of the sanctuary and beckoned the girls to hurry in but to stay together. Tad followed through the narrow opening, using the rock walls for support.

The cave seemed accommodating. Frostbite and hypothermia had taken its toll on all of them. Tad seemed the weakest. He had pleaded with Theresa several times along the journey to leave him behind as he knew he was slowing their progress and potentially risking their lives, but she refused. They all refused.

The children huddled together on the floor of the cave, trying to warm themselves.

Theresa called out to locate the girls and helped Tad over to where they sat shivering.

"Keep an eye on them, won't you, Tad?" she asked, knowing that he really couldn't but wanting to make him feel useful. "I saw some deadwood and kindling just outside the entrance. It'll make a proper fire."

After several minutes, she returned with armfuls of wood and brush. She made several more trips outside to gather wood, each time fearing that when she returned, one or more of them might have succumbed to the cold. She could hear the girls' teeth chattering, but what troubled her more was the silence from Tad.

Theresa felt the ground and cleared the leaves from where the fire would be built. The ground was soft, and her hands went deep into it. Instantly the numerous cuts on her hands and fingers began stinging. "What the hell?" she exclaimed as she pulled her hands from the sand and dusted them off.

Theresa tasted a pinch of the stinging sand. It was a salty sandstone mix.

"Girls!" she called out. "Girls, I want you to dig a trench in the floor! All three of you! Start digging a big trench. A trench big enough in which you all can sit!"

They responded with silence. Only the sound of the howling wind outside could be heard.

"Girls! Did you hear me?" After another moment of silence, Theresa could hear the sound of moving sand. Theresa again withdrew her lighter from her pocket. *Flick, flick, flick.* Then a *crunch, crunch.* The wet flint was breaking into bits. Theresa crumpled to the ground in a ball. She had lost all hope. It was over. They would all die in this dark cave.

"Theresa?" Tad weakly called out. "Theresa?"

She sat back up, trying to regain her composure. "Yes, Tad," she said, choking back the tears.

"Here, try this."

She crawled over to where Tad's voice was coming from. She felt his icy cold face with her hands in the darkness.

Tad grasped her arm and worked his way down to her hand. He placed something in it, something cold and metallic.

"What's this?" she asked.

"It's my pocketknife," he explained. "Find a hard rock and scrape the blade against it. It might spark enough to start the fire."

She felt around the ground for a hard stone. Most of what she found was soft and crumbled in her hand, but she eventually found a hard oval rock. She quickly worked her way back to the pile of kindling with the knife and rock. After crumbling a few handfuls of leaves onto the pile, Theresa opened the blade of the knife, locking it into place.

"T'reeza?" Katie called out in the darkness.

"What?" Theresa snapped in frustration.

"We finished digging the trench! Now whuh?"

Theresa paused for a moment. "Gather as many leaves as you can! Line the trough with them and cover yourselves up! Cover up Tad too! Everyone into the trench and cover yourselves with leaves!"

"Come on, Mr Turly," Hilary said. "Into the trench with you!" The sound of moving leaves rustled in the darkness.

Theresa began scraping the knife blade against the rock. Sparks burst from the rock and blade onto the kindling.

After several moments, smoke could be smelled in the cave. Soon light began revealing their sanctuary.

Theresa stoked the small flame, first with the shredded bark and twigs and then with larger branches. Light and warmth soon filled the chamber.

A sudden wave of exhaustion enveloped her. She had to steady herself from falling, but her mind would have none of it. Not just yet anyway. She and the others had been running on pure adrenaline for much of the day. Now that the emergency had lessened, her body was demanding rest. She was certain that the others felt the same.

"Come on out, everyone!" she said. "It's warm by the fire now, and I want to check your hands and feet for frostbite. We need to get you out of those wet clothes too."

After a moment, Theresa could see the leaves moving in the flickering amber light as Katie and Hilary poked their heads out. Hilary unburied Tad and helped him to his feet. Mina remained in the leaves, motionless.

Theresa quickly moved toward Mina.

"I fink she's sleeping," Katie said nervously as Theresa gently tried to wake her. Mina didn't respond.

"Oh God," Theresa said to herself. "Mina! Wake up, love! Wake up!"

Finally Mina sat up, much to everyone's relief.

"Come over to the fire, Mina. It's warm!"

Mina stared at Theresa. After a moment, she felt her ear.

"I… I can't hear you. I can't hear anything!" she said in a loud, fearful voice.

Theresa grasped her head in her hands and looked directly into Mina's eyes. She spoke slowly, in hope that Mina could read her lips. "It's just the cold, Mina. Once you warm up, you'll be able to hear out of your good ear again. Come over to the fire. I need to make sure you're okay!"

Mina nodded, and Theresa helped her to her feet. One by one, Theresa inspected the others for frostbite. She checked Tad first as he was the oldest and most at risk.

Everyone's ears seemed to be the most affected by the ordeal, but their skin was rapidly turning bright pink as they warmed up. Theresa breathed a long sigh of relief.

The four were none too happy about having to strip down to only their knickers, but Theresa was adamant about it. They timidly hung their wet clothes on long sticks posted into the sand near the fire.

Despite the warmth of the fire, Tad's condition remained critical. He was very pale and was struggling to breathe. Theresa feared pneumonia was setting in.

She used a piece of torn cloth from her coat to clean his head wound. It was a nasty gash and would most certainly leave a scar. Fortunately, the wound had long since clotted, and Tad seemed in no danger from it though he complained of a dreadful headache.

Before stripping off her own wet outer garments, Theresa brought in a pile of snow to be used for quenching their thirst. They had no container to melt it in, so they simply had to nibble and suck on small snowballs from the melting pile.

The cave was warming up nicely though the smoke from the fire stung everyone's eyes and made them cough.

Katie began taking an interest in the little sanctuary that they had found. The walls were rounded and felt like gritty sandpaper to her except for one wall. It was hard and almost looked like quartz. Katie tapped the wall with her fist. A jagged shard fell to the ground, impaling itself in the soft sand just before her feet.

"Snarfflebum!" she muttered aloud, stepping back several steps. Katie looked at the low ceiling above her; it was charred black from fires lit here long ago. They weren't the first ones to have sought refuge here.

Mina and Hilary had buried themselves under dry leaves together to stay warm. Hilary had long since fallen asleep whilst Mina moaned softly and held her hand to her ear.

Several hours had passed, and everyone had re-dressed in their now dry outer garments—except for their coats as they were still damp. Everyone slept for a time except Theresa. She sat watching and thinking, tossing new branches and logs onto the fire to keep it burning brightly.

She'd spread her wet tobacco from the leather pouch onto a rock to dry and was more than ready for a pipeful or two. She fondled the old pipe and felt the strange writing that had been carved into it.

She then turned her attention to Tad. She had unfinished business with this man. She slowly crept over to where he lay. He was awake, but his breathing seemed strained and difficult.

Tad looked over to her as she approached with her freshly lit pipe. She offered it to him; he declined but thanked her anyway. She sat cross-legged next to him in silence.

"I don't know where to start," he said with an apologetic tone and dropping the London accent. His accent was now the same as Mina's.

"How about at the beginning?" she replied flatly.

There was a long silence between them as Tad tried to assemble the right words. Katie, overhearing the conversation, quietly crept over and sat next to Tad.

He began. "I didn't know for certain that it was you until I saw your pipe in the car a couple of days ago. His face contorted uncomfortably. "The pipes, our pipes, are the same because we are from the same place. An old man named Ollie crafted them for us, one for me and one for your father, Edmund, which he passed down to you."

"Edmund," Theresa mumbled to herself as Tad spoke.

"You, me, and Mina. We are all from another place, another world."

Katie's eyes opened wide. "You mean… you're not lowcul?" she said in disbelief. Theresa sat unmoved, staring deep into Tad's eyes.

Tad continued after a deep coughing attack. "Our people are called the Aoileach. We—"

"You're the one. You're the one who told Mina all these horseshit stories, aren't you, Tad?" Theresa interrupted in anger. "You convinced that frail little deaf girl that she's some kind of saviour to this imaginary world of yours, didn't you? You screwed up her head with all these rubbish stories. You bastard."

Tad lay quiet for a moment. "I think in your heart you know this is not horseshit. Now take note. I might not have much time left, and you need to listen to me very carefully."

"How stupid do you think I am?" Theresa was shaking now. "Are you saying we're part mermaid and elf like Mina claims to be?"

Theresa fell silent again. She was trying hard to reject this impossible story, but memory flashes filled her mind in rapid-fire succession. She felt dizzy and overwhelmed.

Tad motioned to her for the pipe. Hesitantly she handed it over. He took a long puff and after a moment looked at the writing on it.

"This pipe was given to your father when he was confirmed an elder. We were all given them. Your father's name and the date of his confirmation are written in Elvish, a people we have great respect for. You are not mer or elf, and neither am I. We are regular folk who coexist in another world…"

"You had no intention of taking us to Cannich, did you, Tad? Where the hell were you taking us? To find this magical world of yours?" Theresa said sharply.

Tad shook his head vehemently. "No, Theresa, that's not true. I lost the map. I must have made a wrong turn. I really was taking the girls to Cannich like we planned… at least Katie and Hilary. The rest of the journey would be up to you and Mina. You must believe me. I wouldn't lie to you."

Theresa was red-faced now. "You wouldn't? What happened to your accent, Tad? That Londoner's accent? One of them is a lie. Oh, and all this rubbish about another world and some stupid prophecy about me are true? Why should I believe anything you say?"

Tad was silent for a moment, contemplating Theresa's words. "I never told you about the prophecy and you being chosen. How did you know about that?"

"It was… it was in my dream," she stammered.

"You didn't tell me about any dream, so how could I have known about it? Who is in this dream?" Tad demanded.

Theresa stared into the old man's eyes. "You… you were very young. And my father. You took me away from my father."

Tad took a deep puff from the pipe and handed it back to Theresa.

"That wasn't a dream, Treena. It's a memory. That really happened almost forty years ago. Does it still sound like horseshit to you now?"

Theresa stood, holding her hands to her face. "This is a nightmare! It has to be, a bloody nightmare! And don't call me Treena! My name is Theresa!"

Tad continued, "I brought you through with me from the other side almost forty years ago. The Augur prophesied you would be the one to return the Hidden Child from exile and that the two of you could restore the light of life to Caledonia."

Hilary poked her head up from the leaves. The argument had

awakened her from her sleep. She prodded Mina awake, and they watched the words flying between Tad and Theresa.

"What are they on about?" Mina whispered in Hilary's ear. Hilary shook her head and shrugged. Mina tried to read both Tad's and Theresa's lips, but in the flickering light, she could only catch bits and pieces. The two of them crept over and seated themselves next to Katie, whose eyes were bloated and unblinking.

"So if this is all true, why did I have to grow up alone in an orphanage, Tad? Did you dump me there after coming through this magical tree? Where the hell have you been all my life if I'm so damned important?" Theresa said, tears glinting on her cheeks in the firelight.

Tad put his head down. "We didn't come here by way of the redwood port. We came by ship, through a portal that has long since closed..."

"A ship? Was it a spaceship, Tad? Was it made by space elves?" Theresa said sarcastically.

"Woods elves," Mina muttered to herself.

"The redwood port," Tad continued, ignoring Theresa's outburst, "is the last portal in existence between the two worlds. All the others are closed; but that one was left open for you and Mina. Several days after we arrived here, you ran off after shooting me with my own rifle. I didn't receive this injury during the war. You shot me out of anger. I searched for you for almost thirty years until I finally gave up."

Theresa felt a charge go through her head like an electrical shock. Horrible memories flashed through her mind: her anger at young Tad, screaming at him for taking her from her family, and finally, the night she pulled his hunting rifle from the tabletop and fired it. She had forgotten these things so very long ago. Those were the memories she had blocked out.

"Oh my God," she said, her hands pressed hard against her temples. "I remember... I remember!" She stumbled about the cave frantically as though looking for a place to hide from the memories that were now assaulting her mind.

Theresa stared at Tad in horror. "I shot you... I wanted my daddy, and you wouldn't let me go home, so I shot you!"

Tad nodded. "I'm not angry about it. I never really was. You were just a child who wanted to go home. I understood that. Now somehow fate has brought us all together again."

"Why didn't you try to take Mina back yourself?" Theresa asked with remorseful tears in her eyes.

Tad shook his head. "The Augur's prophecy was very specific; at the appointed time, you had to be the one to bring Mina home. You are the bridge between worlds."

Theresa searched her mind for the meaning of those strange words. "Augur," she said aloud. "She… she was the old blind woman. She had white eyes."

Tad nodded. "She is long dead now, as are most of the elders of the Aoileach. The Augur gave the prophecy years before you were even born."

"What do you mean, bridge between worlds?"

"Your mother, Miramanee, was from this world, and your father was from Mina's."

"Miramanee… That sounds American Indian."

"Arapaho Indian. The Augur prophesied you would be the one to bring the child home. It *has* to be you, as you are from both worlds. Only you can turn the key."

"Why?" Theresa asked.

"Your DNA is from both worlds," Katie said. "Mina's key probably requires bits of you from both worlds for access. Bits from each realm. It's like needing a special password to get into a certain kind of pub. No password, no entry. No, wait… terrible analogy. Forget I said pub."

Tad and Theresa gave Katie an odd look before continuing.

"And Mina's part?" Theresa asked.

Tad nodded again. "Her birth and part in all this was given many years before that. *The Hidden Child will be born of mer and elf, frail and fair. Her lifeblood will end the Wasting, but be warned. She brings the Daemose. The two heads will become one. Guundalin will be loosed.*"

"What does all that mean?" Theresa asked. Her head had begun to spin. She carefully sank to a sitting position on the cave floor.

Tad shook his head. "I don't know for certain. No one does, but Mina somehow has the cure to the plague that has been killing our people for many years and the Daemose is believed to be an evil entity that lives within a human and brings chaos and death."

"A demon?"

"Not just a demon but the *Daemon*. It would be the equivalent of the devil. Satan."

"What about the two heads?"

"I have no idea about that one, Theresa."

"And Guundalin?"

Tad shook his head. "Don't know."

"You don't actually think Mina is this Daemose or Guundalin, do you?" Theresa whispered, trying to hide her mouth from Mina.

"Of course not! But the prophecy says she brings it with her. What that means, I don't know, but Mina is innocent."

"She's not a *bàs aislingeach*?"

A look of concern covered Tad's face. "Where did you hear…?"

"Erm," said Katie. "I 'ate to mention this roight now, but there are eyes in the dark."

Chapter forty five

Dance of Shadows

EVERYONE TURNED TO see what Katie was on about. Eyes. There were five pale blue eyes moving in the shadows, the light of the fire reflecting in their pupils.

"Theresa, put some more wood on the fire... slowly," Tad commanded as he struggled to his feet. "Hilary, bring me those two long sticks that the jackets are hanging on... slowly. No sudden moves." He carefully reached down to the rock where his pocketknife was lying open and retrieved it.

Two sets of eyes and a single eye were now staring at them. As the fire grew brighter, the waning shadows revealed three enormous wet wolves. Their eyes fixed on their potential meals.

Mina now stood watching the huge beasts. "Basil dogs!" she exclaimed as she moved toward them. "Hi, dogs!"

Tad grasped her by the shoulder and shook his head at her. "Bad dogs!" he said. "Stay behind me! All of you stay behind me!"

Hilary handed the long sticks to Tad, her hands shaking. "Are they going to eat us, Mr Turly?"

"Girls," Theresa said, motioning with her hand. "I want all of you in that corner."

Katie curled her lip. "Tha's the corner we've been using as a toilet!"

"Move it, you lot. No lip. In the corner."

Hilary took Mina by the hand and led her to the back of the cave. They clenched hands as they watched the creatures slowly circling the cavern.

Tad worked quickly, cutting the bark from the ends of both sticks, fashioning them into double-edged spears.

"Is that the last of the firewood?" he said, his eyes fixed on the animals.

Theresa slowly inched her way back to Tad's side without blinking, her eyes also on them. "That's it."

Tad handed the first spear to Theresa. She carefully felt the sharpened tips without moving her eyes from the wild dogs; they would do nicely.

"Where the hell are we, Tad?" Theresa demanded.

"What do you mean?"

"Tad, there are no wolves in Scotland. Where are we?"

"I don't think they're local," he responded. Katie blinked several times at his use of her catchphrase.

The one-eyed beast's empty socket appeared to be staring at Theresa. The wolves separated and slowly positioned themselves where the gap between the fire and walls was the widest.

"We have two spears and three wolves to deal with. I want you to stay with the girls. You will be the last line of defence," Tad said in a monotone voice.

"No!" Theresa protested. "You can't handle all three of them!"

"No, I can't. But I *can* get two of them. It will be up to you to get the last one if she gets through. The dog with one eye will be the last to attack. She'll be the one you'll have to deal with. Keep to her blind side."

Theresa stepped backwards toward the shaking girls, her spear in hand, her eyes fixed on the wolves. She looked at Tad before her, who now stood tall, with his spear readied, towering over the wild dogs.

They waited. Soon the fire died down. There was now room for the beasts to cross by the fire, but the wolves waited.

As the last log began sputtering, the cavern darkened, and the dance of shadows began.

Two of the grey wolves approached from Tad's right, along the wall, and the other from his left. They seemed more like shadows in the night moving against the walls. As the darkness swallowed the light, all anyone could see was the glow of eyes. Growls and snarling sounds replaced the silence. Tad began screaming at the beasts and waving his arms, hoping that they would flee in fear; they didn't even flinch.

Suddenly a bit of light leapt from the smouldering fire as the last log rolled over in the collapsing ash. The backside of the wood had not yet burned but was now exposed to the sparks and small bits of unburned kindling. The flickering light was sporadic, but the others could see the silhouette of Tad moving with incredible speed and precision.

Tad's shadow struck with his spear and continued striking the shadows that approached. The stop-action motion from the sputtering flames created a surreal image.

The two beasts' shadows then separated. As they launched themselves in a final fury, Tad broke his spear into two over his thigh. With lightning speed, he thrust one into the heart of the first wolf and the other into the second wolf's underbelly as the beast crashed down upon him. Tad collapsed under its weight in silence and shadow as the last of the light was extinguished from the cave.

Theresa took several steps backward toward the girls in the blackness. The only sound she could hear was her own heartbeat and the girls hyperventilating in fear. Theresa readied her spear, but to what end? She couldn't see anything. She held her breath, hoping to remove the sound of her own breathing. She felt something touch her waist and turned suddenly.

"It's just me!" Hilary cried out as Theresa prepared to strike.

Silence again filled the cave, with only strange echoes reverberating around the cavern, the echoes of an animal panting nearby. After a moment, Theresa could smell the wet coat of the dog now at her feet. A growl rose up to her ears as she squeezed her spear tightly whilst turning it downward. The animal leapt onto her, knocking her to the ground. As the girls screamed in terror, Theresa thrust the spear toward it. The spear suddenly felt heavy and crashed to the ground, ripped from Theresa's grasp.

Silence filled the cavern.

"Is… is everyone okay?" Theresa finally said. The girls began sobbing. Theresa hesitantly reached through the darkness until she found the end of the spear. With trembling hands, she ran her fingers to the other end of the spear, terrified of what lay on the other end.

The spear ran through the dog's hollow eye socket and out the back of its head.

It twitched horribly for some time.

It was over.

46 Chapter forty Six

Final Words

THERESA PULLED THE spear from the wolf's head and crawled over to where the smouldering fire lay. She snapped it into several pieces and placed them among the embers. After a long moment, she crawled over to where she last saw Tad.

Tad lay in a crumpled pile as Theresa and the girls approached. Theresa gently placed her hand on his bloodied shoulder. She wasn't sure if the blood belonged to Tad or the wolves.

She gently rolled him onto his back. He smiled sadly as she caressed his face. Tears dripped from her eyes onto his cheek. He didn't seem to mind.

"Are we safe?" he whispered. The other girls knelt beside him as well, tears streaming down their faces.

Theresa, choking back a sob, nodded. "You saved us, Tad. We are still alive, thanks to you."

"I… I don't think I'll be going with you to Cannich," he whispered.

"Nonsense," Theresa said with a false, quivering smile. "We need you to get us home to Balynfirth."

Tad's eyes were growing dim. Hilary covered her mouth with one hand and squeezed Mina's hand with the other. Katie was visibly shaking.

"Listen to the trees, Theresa. They will show you the way," he said, his voice so weak she could barely hear him. "Mina knows the language. She can help you."

"Mina's deaf, Tad. She can't hear anything," Theresa said, sobbing.

"You can't hear them… you can't hear them with… feel them. Mina… Mina can teach you… Father would be so proud…" Tad didn't finish. His eyes grew blank and motionless. He was gone.

Theresa clasped her hands to her face and began sobbing. Katie and Hilary knelt down, wrapping their arms around her. They wept in each other's arms as the waning light flickered and sputtered.

Mina knelt before Tad. She gazed at his face for a long moment in silence. Mina placed her two fingers first to her forehead and then onto Tad's brow. She uttered some words in Old Elvish. Tad's eyes gently closed, and a soft smile covered his face. He was at peace.

The cave had grown dark and quiet except for the occasional sputter and spark of the dying embers. Katie shivered as the cold had reclaimed the cavern.

Hilary watched Theresa, who sat motionless next to Tad, lost in her own thoughts and grief. She crept over to Katie. Hilary motioned to her to follow. They silently put on their nearly dry jackets and shoes. After pulling the two spears from the beasts Tad had killed, they moved toward the exit of the cave, carefully peering out the opening for any more wolves. Shortly they returned with more wood and kindling from outside. They made several more trips for wood, stacking it neatly in a pile near the far wall of the cave.

Mina watched, shivering in silence as the two girls refuelled the fire with dead wood. Smoke rose from the embers, and soon the fire was blazing again, its warmth filling the cavern.

Hilary gently covered Tad's face and upper body with his coat. It was a black woollen coat that would have helped keep the girls warm, but she wasn't ready to consider that now.

She then took Theresa's coat and draped it over the mourning woman's shoulders and back.

Hilary handed Mina her jacket, and along with Katie, they quietly buried themselves in the leaves to try to sleep.

Chapter Forty Seven

The Dark Day

THERESA AROSE AND approached the fattest of the dead wolves. With Tad's knife, she began cutting the skin and fur from the body of the beast. She laid the animal skin, fur side down, on the ground and cut chunks of flesh from the carcass.

With her hands covered in blood, Theresa placed the wolf meat onto three long sticks and secured them into the ground above the fire.

Whilst the meat cooked, she did the same to the other wolves' carcasses, carefully removing their skins in one piece. Theresa scraped the blood from the skins with Tad's knife and rubbed them in a circular motion with a smooth chunk of rock salt she had pried from a nearby wall until it began dissolving. This would preserve the skins and keep the children warm. She laid them near the fire to dry. With the cold temperatures, the food would last several days. She didn't relish the idea of eating wolf, but faced with starvation, she was sure even the girls would agree that it was a godsend. Theresa then ground the remaining salt into powder and applied it liberally to the meat. After placing the meat on a piece of cloth and sampling a bit of it, Theresa lay down next to Tad and finally, mercifully, fell asleep.

It was early afternoon before the girls awoke. Filtered light invaded the cave from outside. The late spring storm had ended, leaving deep snowdrifts under a mostly cloudy sky. The sound of melting snow dripping onto the ground from the cave entrance could be heard. Their eyes grew wide with excitement when they crawled out of the leaf pile to find the meat that Theresa had prepared for them. Then the reality of where it came from struck them.

They stared at the food as Theresa slept next to Tad's cold body.

Hilary finally spoke up. "I know it's a disgusting thing to think about, eating this, but we have to. We'll starve if we don't. Theresa went to great lengths to prepare it for us, and I think Mr Turly would insist that we eat it as well."

With that, Hilary pulled a chunk of the stringy meat from the pile and began eating. Shortly Katie and Mina followed her lead.

After taking their fill, Hilary and Katie began digging a grave in the sand for Tad whilst Mina gathered more wood and stoked the fire to warm and light the dimly lit cave. She also brought in a huge pile of snow for drinking, setting it near the entrance.

Hilary and Katie often broke into tears and would have to stop until the wave of grief had passed over them. Mina showed little emotion but would often come to a complete standstill in whatever she was doing and spend a long moment staring blankly at nothing, in a trancelike state. They each grieved in their own way.

Finally the task was complete. The three girls struggled to drag Turly into the shallow grave. Theresa awoke to the sound and bade the girls to stop.

"Just give me a moment," she said, still not quite awake.

After a time, Theresa rose and helped them place Tad in his final resting place. They all sat silently, lost in their own thoughts.

After several minutes, Theresa pulled the heavy winter coat from Tad's body and replaced it with a torn piece of cloth from the lining of her own coat; they would need it. She also slipped his pipe into its coat pocket.

Mina said some words over the grave in Old Elvish as Theresa, Katie, and Hilary covered Tad with the soft sand. None of them understood their meaning, but the words seemed appropriate nonetheless.

After viewing the position of the sun in the sky, Theresa decided they would spend one more night in the cave and head out in the morning, rested.

Using Tad's knife, they took turns sharpening sticks into stakes and spears. The stakes were then wedged into the gaps of the rock barrier to discourage any animal from entering. There was now scarcely a place for a wolf to enter the cave without stepping on a sharp stick and injuring its feet or puncturing its underbelly or face. The longer spears were just in case they got past the barrier.

Theresa spotted Mina sitting near the fire, pushing a slab of the cold meat onto a stick with a look of disgust on her face. Mina thrust the stick into the fire to heat it. Shortly the greasy meat caught fire. Theresa watched in amusement as the girl's eyes grew wide as she tried to deal with the flaming torch of meat before her. Mina, in a panic, was eventually able to blow out the flames and gnaw on the charred wolf meat. Afterward, Theresa wrapped the remaining meat in a bit of cloth and packed it in snow. They would need it.

It was late evening when the silence of the cave and the reassuring sound of the fire were interrupted by the wolves. Mina, with closed eyes, began singing, an eerie, haunting chant, which lasted for several hours whilst the wolves attempted to enter the cave. The others took comfort and joined in Mina's song though they didn't understand the words. They imagined it to be some type of protective spell.

Occasional yelps and howls could be heard as the wolves repeatedly injured themselves on the sharp sticks and long spears protecting the winding entrance. A fight erupted outside the cave, and Katie guessed that one or more of the injured animals may have wound up as a meal for the others.

The three girls eventually crawled into their leaf trough and fell asleep, snuggling close together for warmth.

Theresa took watch with spears ready in case one of the hungry wolves broke through the barrier.

She paced the cave and stoked the fire. She pulled her pipe from her trouser pocket. As was her habit, she looked long at the strange writing on its surface. To her surprise, she could now read it:

Edmund Turly: Elder, 34th Janar, 1220.

The meaning of these words slapped Theresa across the face. Her surname was Turly. She had been assigned a last name at Saint Austin's, like many of the orphans. *Ward*. But she had never known her real name until now. Theresa was a Turly, and Tad, her uncle. She wished she had known sooner.

She wondered if there were still some Turlys in Balynfirth. What would her father think of her if he were still alive and they met now? And what of her mother? That remained a mystery to her. Soon, however, her mind stilled, and she drifted off to sleep, her back to a large rock, spear in hand. The siren's song played in her mind as she dreamed of home.

Meanwhile, Mina's dreams were filled with a disjointed and disturbing collage of rapid-fire images. Her monochromatic nightmare took place in total silence, and even though she could see the faces of people talking and screaming, she couldn't hear their words or make any sense of what she was seeing or experiencing.

A cabin that appears and disappears. A cavern with long, narrow, steep stairs, so steep that the fear of falling comes with each downward step into the darkness. The horrible stench of stagnant water and an old ship with tattered sails where death awaits to claim its victims. The black water... something about black water...

Mina finds herself walking alone in the empty moors, the chilly rain soaking her to the bone. She seems to be moving in slow motion. The silent voices of distant trees beckoning her to run and then mourning as it is now too late. Her hair is matted to her head and face, her unfocused eyes fixed on the ground before her.

Blurred and violent movements all about her, from a horrible form that is bent on her destruction. Blood, so much blood. The deafening sound of silence and loneliness. Tears mixed with mud, running down her face onto the ground below.

The source of the violence then becomes clear—those bulging, angry, red eyes and that sneering, cruel mouth with brown teeth. The horrible energy and smell this man gives off, so poisonous, so cruel. Mina can feel the beat of her own heart pounding, pulsing through her body, down to the end of her fingertips. A single word enters her ears in a whisper. "Mina…" She turns her head toward the sound of someone calling her name.

"Mina! Wake up! Wake up!" Katie said frantically, shaking her.

Mina opened her eyes. Hilary and Katie were sitting next to her in the bed of leaves, Hilary's hand on her shoulder.

Mina sat up quickly and looked about the cave, blinking, unsure of which vision was real. She turned back to Hilary.

"You all right?" Hilary asked with concern.

Mina shook her head, her eyes wild with fear, filling with tears.

"Whuh did you see?" Katie asked.

"He is going to kill me… that man…"

Morning arrived. The girls packed what they could carry as Theresa pulled the sharpened wooden stakes and spears from the ground. Many were covered in dried blood and bits of fur and skin from the wolves' failed attempts to enter the cave the night before.

Theresa carefully wrapped as many of the longer spears and stakes as she could into the remaining strips of wolf skin and bound them securely to carry. Each girl had a wolf blanket to cover herself, with several ties sewn in on each side to keep the wind out. The blankets covered the girls like ponchos, though they had to wear them fur-side in as the skins weren't yet cured.

Theresa now donned Tad's woollen coat over her own. It was huge on her, and she wept a bit as she fastened the remaining buttons, but she knew Tad would have insisted that she wear it.

Katie, taking Mina by the arm, demanded that she share her dream with Theresa. Mina hesitantly shared the details of her nightmare.

Theresa dwelled upon the girl's vision in silence. *Was there a way to prevent the confrontation? Perhaps by avoiding the landmarks that Mina described… or were these events already set in time and unavoidable, no matter what path they chose?* Theresa had no answer. But they couldn't stay here any longer. If the cold weather stayed on, the wolf meat would last several days. If it warmed above freezing, the meat would spoil, and they would go hungry. She was also becoming very concerned for Mina, who was now feverish and quite pale. She needed to find help for the girl soon.

Theresa tested her lighter to see if the flint was dry. *Flick.* It worked. She sighed in relief.

The sky was growing overcast. The ground was peppered with several wolf carcasses, their blood staining the snow.

They had not seen their surroundings until now. The blizzard that had brought them here had made that quite impossible. They paused to take in the view. It was spectacular and yet daunting and ever so lonely. To the west, below the rock formation they stood upon, a vast moorland opened up before them.

"Well, let's get a move on!" Katie proclaimed in her usual cheerful manner.

Mina didn't move. She stood silent, her eyes following the swaying branches of the trees that surrounded them. She closed her eyes. She seemed to be listening.

"Mina?" Theresa asked, forgetting the little girl's deafness. Then she remembered Tad's final words. She gently placed her hand on Mina's shoulder. Mina's tear-filled eyes met hers. "Which way should we go, love?"

"This way. We're supposed to go this way," Mina said with a trembling voice and quivering bottom lip as she pointed to the valley below.

Theresa nodded in silence to Mina, pulling her close. She slowly loaded her supply pack onto her still-sore shoulder, wincing slightly.

"All right, you lot! Let's go!" she said with a false cheerfulness in her voice.

They carefully descended the rocks into the valley below.

The moors awaited them.

End of Book Two

Acknowledgements

Very special thanks to those who helped make this book possible:

Mumm's the Word Editorial Services:

Anita Mumm, you are amazing! Thank you for your incredible developmental edits and for teaching me the craft of writing. I have a long way to go, but your efforts were life changing and I am grateful for you and your patience with me.

Victory Editing:

Anne, Annie, Tami and Linda, thank you for your awesome line-editing work and prep for publication. I couldn't have done this without you! (I could have, but it would have been total rubbish.) Thank you so very much! I am so grateful to you.

Creative Paramita Book Cover Artist:

Paramita Bhattacharjee, your cover design brought to life the story and its spirit. I even changed the colour of Theresa's scarf to maroon, as your image was so much better than what I had written! I smile with joy every time I look at it. Thank you!

I also wish to thank several musicians, as their music was a direct influence and inspiration to the story:

Loreena McKennitt:

Her studio version of "Prospero's Speech" was the inspiration for the siren's song. I visualise Lir rising from the water, singing this song to seduce her prey.

The studio version of "Huron 'Beltane' Fire Dance," was the inspiration for the song that Theresa was so desperately trying to remember; the song that awakened the spirit of the trees and harbingers.

Mac Davis:

"Whoever Finds This, I Love You," *inspired the scene wherein Old Turly meets Mina.*

Jon Mark:

"Perilous and Mystical Journey," *was the inspiration for the scene wherein Theresa is standing before her daughter's grave and her gazing at the wintery surroundings, after sliding off the road in her car.*

Thank you all,
MK Shevlin

Printed in Great Britain
by Amazon

38386137R00128